RING OF FIVE

A Novella and Four Stories

Also by F.H. Thurmond

Before I Sleep: A Memoir of Travel and Reconciliation

Et Alia Press, 2012

RING OF FIVE
A NOVELLA AND FOUR STORIES

F.H. THURMOND

et alia press

Little Rock, Arkansas 2015

www.EtaliaPress.com

© F.H. Thurmond 2015

Published in the United States of America by
Et Alia Press
  1819 Shadow Lane
  Little Rock, AR
  72207

ISBN 978-0-9828184-6-6

Cover & Text Design: Jeremy Kistler

A shorter version of "The Call" was previously published in
Best of Tales from the South: Volume 6, edited by Paula Martin
Morell and Stephanie Trevino Slagle. North Little Rock:
Temenos Press, 2012.

CONTENTS

For my mother, Barbara H. Thurmond,
in gratitude for the love of stories.

THE DEALER'S TALE

Now, goode men, God foryeve yow youre trespas,
And ware yow fro the synne of avarice.
            —Geoffrey Chaucer, "The Pardoner's Tale"

THE AFTERNOON HAZE shimmered obliquely among
downtown high-rises as Miller and Reeve crossed the
old art deco bridge over the LA River. Canal rather, as the
river was long ago transformed into a network of concrete
canals boasting a mere trickle of dirty water where the river once flowed. But neither this nor the faded glory of the
city's past—to which the bridge hearkened as a crumbling re-
minder—crossed either man's mind as they approached the
pot-holed streets lined with empty, graffiti-laden warehouses
beyond the canal.

Miller, the older man, was driving, as they both stared
straight ahead with inscrutable expressions. Reeve caught a
peripheral glimpse of something floating through the air just

beneath the bridge. It appeared to be a bird with multi-hued plumes; then he saw a young Asian boy run forward to catch it with an outstretched hand. The boy looked up at the car as it reached the bridge's edge, and his and Reeve's eyes met for a moment before Miller turned and rounded a sharp corner between two dilapidated warehouses. Reeve stared back curiously.

The boy strolled with his toy bird along the river canal, until he abruptly stopped and looked ahead at something moving beneath the bridge. There he saw a strange figure, cloaked in a dark trench coat, moving around mysteriously under the archway. He appeared to be burying something with rocks, before quickly slipping away and disappearing down the train tracks running along the canal.

Miller appeared restless as he drove, running his dirty fingers through his long, greasy hair. He shot Reeve a quick look.

"I should be back in Vegas, dealing out cards."

Reeve glared at him with contempt. "Instead of here, dealing out death?"

Miller stared ahead in silence a moment. "That guy got what he deserved."

Reeve appeared suddenly disgusted. "Who are you to judge that? Is a little money worth a man's life?"

"For the love of Christ, man!"

Reeve stared at Miller angrily. "I asked you to stop swearing in the Lord's name."

Miller flashed Reeve a sanctimonious smile. "Look, if he'd simply paid up, he'd have got a full pardon."

"Who could ever pardon you?" Reeve muttered. Miller slammed on the brakes and the car screeched to a stop.

"What's your problem, anyway?"

Reeve sighed. "This is seriously fucked up."

"What is?"

"Your so-called *methods*."

"I'm just doing my job," Miller grumbled. "*Our* job, remember?"

Reeve shook his head in disbelief at his fate. "Why did I ever come out here? This was supposed to be about drama…"

"You can't say this ain't dramatic now, can you?"

Reeve suppressed a reply, and they both sat staring angrily ahead until a loud horn broke the silence. Miller looked in the rearview mirror and saw a small car behind, its driver gesticulating impatiently. He punched the gas pedal and tore off furiously, then turned into an empty street and slowed to a stop in front of a large trash dumpster. The two men got out of the car at the same instant and slammed the doors in unison. Miller left the keys in the ignition, while the once posh Mercedes continued to idle with an annoying rattle. Miller banged the hood with his fist, and the rattle momentarily stopped before resuming again even louder. "Piece of shit!" Miller scowled.

The men moved toward the rear of the car and Miller reached to unlock the trunk. A church bell began to toll somewhere in the distance, and Reeve looked up thoughtfully.

"*For whom the bell tolls*, right?"

Miller frowned as he opened the trunk. "Yeah, but why sit around waiting for the inevitable?"

Reeve glanced at the contents of the trunk and shook his head in disgust.

"Better to find Death first," concluded Miller. "Confront him face to face."

Reeve glared at Miller. "You want to find Death? Just look in the mirror."

"Very funny."

The church bell continued to echo in the distance as the men strained to lift something heavy from the trunk: a large body wrapped in layers of black garbage bags like a mummy, which they now carried toward the open dumpster. As they heaved the body into the dumpster, an old line of verse learned in school popped into Reeve's head. *"Each of us become the others' brother, and we will slay this false traitor Death."*

"Shakespeare!" exclaimed Miller excitedly.

Reeve shook his head no. "Chaucer."

Annoyed, Miller closed the lid with a loud clang. "Guess we finally put the lid on that asshole." Miller headed back to the car, but Reeve hesitated, staring back at the dumpster. "We? No, *you!*" Both men paused and regarded each other intently.

"It never ends with you, does it?" Reeve continued.

"Ends?"

Reeve pointed at the dumpster. "This!"

Miller slammed the car trunk shut and shot a furious gaze at Reeve as he walked back towards him.

"What the *fuck* do you care about some dealer you didn't even know? How about the thousands of human beings dying in the world every day you never even say a word about? Or do you really give a damn about the suffering you don't see?"

Reeve did not answer, and they headed back to the car in angry silence. But as they started to get in, a toy bird, the same one they had seen earlier, suddenly fluttered toward them and landed on the hood of the car. Both men froze and looked at each other, and then to the street. Reeve found himself staring once again into the young boy's eyes he'd seen at the bridge. Now the boy watched them with a strange expression that unsettled the two men. They looked at each other nervously, then again at the boy. Miller slowly picked up the bird and walked toward him. Observing his partner's mischievous grin, Reeve paused.

"What do we do now?"

Miller looked quickly back at Reeve. "What do you think?" He moved closer to the boy, still grinning while glancing furtively up and down the street as he reached inside his jacket.

"No!" Reeve shouted.

Miller ignored him. He pulled out a dagger and slowly approached the boy with it, while behind him Reeve shrugged and looked at the ground in resignation. But the boy remained calm and still, staring at Miller with a bemused expression, perhaps some mysterious insight. This forced the man to hesitate as his grin slowly faded into doubt. Then the boy spoke.

"I know what you're looking for," he said.

Miller looked back at Reeve and they exchanged curious looks before Miller returned his gaze to the boy. "You know what, kid?"

"I know where you can find what you're looking for."

The men again looked at each other curiously, and Miller slowly withdrew the dagger as he eyed the boy.

A few minutes later Miller slouched behind the wheel again, watching the boy in the rear view mirror. He sat in the back seat, his hands tied but his expression still uncannily relaxed. Reeve held the bird toy in his lap and stared at it in silence; then he abruptly reached up and turned on the radio, adjusting the dial until finding a song he liked. The men each took swigs from a bottle of mescal, and Miller offered the boy a drink. The boy shook his head and Miller handed the bottle back to Reeve and stared at a burnt out row of warehouses ahead.

"This place is hell on earth," he observed.

Reeve appeared suddenly thoughtful. "*The mind is its own place, and in itself, can make a heaven of Hell, and a hell of Heaven.*"

Miller looked at him quizzically. "Shakespeare?"

"Milton."

"Goddammit!"

The car came to a stop near the graffiti-covered bridge and they all got out. The boy led the men to a pile of rocks beneath the bridge, next to a makeshift homeless shelter. A folded blanket indicated a recent tenant. He pointed at the pile and then at the men, observing them with his wry expression. They looked at each other and with a nod quickly removed the rocks until the smooth surface of a large garbage bag glistened in the sun. They excitedly removed it from where it was buried in a shallow hole, before Miller made a small slit in the bag and scooped out a fistful of white powder with his hand. He watched with amazement as it ran through his fingers, cautiously tasting the substance before flashing Reeve a greedy grin. "This is the real thing, all right. White gold!"

Reeve's jaw dropped. "I've never seen so much stash!"

Miller glanced at him gleefully. "*Now* you don't seem so worried about the guy in the garbage. We've just found paradise, man!"

Reeve hesitated. "Or hell…"

"You wanted your fortune and here it is, wrapped up like a gift under a tree." Miller stared at the bag with lusty eyes. "It's Christmas, and it's snowing in LA!"

Reeve looked up concerned. "But what'll we do with all this coke?"

"Sell it man," answered Miller, distractedly. "We can hide it at my place." He saw Reeve shoot him a suspicious look, and quickly added, "Or yours, or yours… It don't matter where we keep it. Then it's back to Vegas baby, and booze, babes, and blackjack galore!"

"So what about the kid?" They looked at the boy, who had sat down between the bridge and the bag of cocaine. His toy bird sat nearby.

"The kid stays here," Miller answered. He drew out the dagger and laid it on a rock near the bag of cocaine. The boy watched as Miller drained the bottle of mescal and aimlessly tossed it aside.

"We need some more booze."

"Are you crazy?" Reeve stared at his partner incredulously. "We gotta get this stuff outta here!"

"No, too much traffic on the bridge, we'll have to chill out till dark. If anyone sees us with all this shit, they'll hang us."

"What if the owner comes back?"

"Fuck 'em, I'll deal with 'em!"

Reeve gestured impatiently as Miller took a joint from his shirt pocket and lit it. "Lighten up dude," he croaked, holding in the smoke. "Let's drink and be merry! How about you go get more booze?"

"How about *you* go?" insisted Reeve, annoyed.

"How 'bout we flip for it instead? Deal?"

"All right. Deal."

Miller took out a quarter, tossed the coin up high and slapped it down on his wrist. He looked up at Reeve to call it.

"Tails!"

Miller slowly uncovered the quarter and saw it was tails. At that moment a siren passed overhead and they both looked up and watched until it quickly passed and faded away across the bridge. When Reeve looked back Miller was smiling and holding out his wrist.

"Heads."

Reeve flashed him a knowing look, but said nothing as Miller tossed him the car keys. Reeve caught them and walked toward the car with a scowl. Behind him Miller's friendly smile quickly disappeared.

Reeve got in the car and slammed the door, then looked back towards Miller and observed the malice in his expression. *"Where we are, there's daggers in men's smiles,"* he said to himself, then started the car and tore away in a cloud of dirty gravel.

Miller stood near the cocaine and stared at the boy thoughtfully. To an onlooker, Miller might have appeared as some hulking troll lurking in silhouette beneath the bridge. He sat down on a large level rock, picked up the dagger lying before him, and began carving out lines of cocaine. When he had three lines neatly spaced apart, he took a bill from his wallet and rolled it into a slender tube. The boy watched as Miller took a deep breath, held the tip of the bill to the first line, and inhaled all three lines with one snort. Then he lit a joint and sat in silence for some time, staring at the huge bag of coke. He froze as a freight train appeared from nowhere and rumbled by along the canal, and it was because of this that he didn't notice Reeve pull up behind him— who now sat observing Miller as he picked up the toy bird and attempted without success to fly it.

In the car Reeve held up a new bottle of mescal and turned it upside down. As he observed the worm drift slowly downwards inside the bottle, his reflection in the glass made his face appear gaunt beneath his thinning hair and dull eyes. He opened the bottle and positioned it upright in his lap as he took out an unlabeled bottle of pills from his jacket pocket;

he opened it and gently shook until a small pill landed in his palm. He lifted his hand to drop the pill into the bottle, but then hesitated a moment as he looked up toward Miller in the distance.

"*Drink off this potion...*" he murmured.

Miller appeared to have lost interest in the toy bird. He tossed it listlessly toward the bridge and then watched as it floated down in circles like a vulture, finally coming to rest on top of the garbage bag. He inhaled again deeply from the joint and stared at the cocaine. When Reeve appeared quietly from behind and slapped him on the shoulder, he jumped up startled.

"Relax man, it's just me! Here, look what I've brought for you." Reeve opened the bottle and handed it to Miller, who promptly set it down on the flat rock behind them. Reeve frowned.

"And look what I've prepared for you!" Miller gestured toward the rock, on which there were several lines of cocaine neatly carved out. Reeve looked at the lines dismayed, but Miller slapped him on the back.

"Let's party dude, there's plenty to spare. We're rich now!" Reeve shrugged and stooped to snort the first line as Miller watched. "What would Shakespeare say now?" he chuckled.

Reeve sniffed and wiped his nose, staring thoughtfully at the toy bird resting against the bags. "*There's a special providence in the fall of a sparrow,*" he answered. As Reeve bent down again over the second line, he caught a glimpse of the boy's alarmed expression, directed toward Miller. Reeve swung around just in time to see Miller lunge at him with the dagger, and he stepped back with the quickness of a torero and grabbed Miller's wrist. "Stab *me* in the back, will you!" he shouted, twisting Miller's arm with a power that belied his small frame. The dagger dropped from Miller's hand and landed directly between the boy and the cocaine. But Miller quickly overpowered Reeve, pinning him down with one hand while with the other he deftly grasped a large rock that had formed part of the pile over the bags. As Miller held the rock aloft and aimed it squarely at his friend's crown, he spotted Reeve's pleading expression. It gave him momentary pause, as something welled up within him he fought bitterly to suppress—a spark of rare feeling, or a hint of conscience long neglected. But a glance at the pile of coke, heaped like a dragon's plunder behind them, quickly dispelled any inkling of repentance as he swung the rock downward at Reeve's skull.

Miller walked nonchalantly over to the lines of cocaine he had carved for Reeve and sniffed them up in one long snort. Then he settled back on the rock, took out a joint, and lit it. As he inhaled, he looked toward the boy, who seemed completely unperturbed by the violence, even though he stared at Reeve's lifeless body, sprawled beside the cocaine with his head face down in mud and blood.

"What's your name, boy?"

"Jeffrey." The boy did not look away from Reeve's body as he answered.

Miller exhaled and looked at Jeffrey.

"I think I've seen you somewhere before." He reached out and picked up the toy bird, which lay next to Reeve's bloody head. "So, Jeffrey, what's the deal with this thing anyway?"

Jeffrey remained silent, as Miller again tried to fly the bird without success. He angrily tossed it up and kicked at it. "Fuck it!" Miller looked up at the downtown skyline and squinted.

He puffed upon the joint as he looked back at Jeffrey. Then he sat down and stared at Reeve's body. A look of sudden bewilderment clouded his eyes with tears, and he put his head in his hands.

"Christ, who could ever pardon what I've done?"

"You've found what you were looking for," came the boy's voice in reply. For a moment, Miller looked both puzzled and hesitant, as he glanced from Reeve's body to the cocaine and then back toward the boy. Finally he just shook his head with an air of resignation, stroking his scraggly beard as he stared across the river.

"*I am in blood stepped in so far that, should I wade no more, returning were as tedious as go o'er.*" He glared at Reeve. "There's your Shakespeare!" he mumbled drily. He picked up the bottle of mescal, opened it, and held it up to the boy's mouth. "Here kid, take a swig. It'll make this easier." Jeffrey slowly shook his head.

"Suit yourself." Miller jerked back the bottle and took a huge swig as he regarded the hole in which the stash had been buried. "This hole's big enough for the both of you." He gestured with the bottle in a mock toast at Reeve's body and took another huge gulp. Setting down the bottle, he picked up the dagger, and slowly moved toward the boy.

But just as he reached out to stab him, Miller abruptly dropped the knife and grimaced in a spasm of sharp pain. He held up the bottle and looked from it to Reeve in disbelief, then staggered backwards gasping for breath before tripping over Reeve's body and falling headfirst into the cocaine. With a last final gasp, he grabbed at the bag and watched with despair as the powder sifted through his fingers. Then there was silence.

The boy quickly freed his hands by rubbing his bonds against Miller's knife, which he held against a rock with his foot. He lifted the large plastic bag of cocaine and slung it over his shoulder and walked towards the river. When he reached the bank of the trickling water, he held the bag out over it and shook vigorously. A cool breeze stirred at that moment, and a cloud of white powder billowed upwards and drifted into the stream.

Jeffrey walked slowly back to the rocks and found his colorful toy between the bodies of the two men. He tossed the bird high in the air out over the river, and watched thoughtfully as it drifted away in the cloudy water.

WHISKEY ROAD

THE SNOW ALREADY lay thick on the road when Carlisle came veering down it, stone blind drunk just after midnight, and hit the brakes of his pickup at the corner of Whiskey Road and Easy Street. His truck spun wildly towards Zack Terry's driveway, where Zack's vintage Harley Davidson now sat under its tarp awaiting a cruel fate. The truck took a perpendicular route across the Terry yard before sliding, sideways, directly into the Harley. The impact produced a spectacularly loud *thump* amid a smattering of flying snow and glass, followed by an abrupt silence.

Carlisle sat for what seemed an infinite moment hunched over the wheel in a daze, until he vaguely became aware of porch lights switching on, illumining the snow-carpeted lawns up and down the road. He heard a door slam nearby and startled voices approached. One of the voices had the unmistakable rasp of Zack Terry. He became aware of a searing emptiness welling up from within his stomach, a sudden piercing levity afflicting his innards—not a physical wound but something else, that familiar gut feeling always indicative of serious trouble. As the fog of intoxication swirling around his eyes quickly dissipated into frightening clarity, he caught another all-too familiar sound: The Doppler whine of an approaching siren.

Carlisle remained frozen where he sat slumped over the wheel, only dimly aware of the spent airbag's acrid fumes swirling about his truck cab. Somebody now pulled frantically at the driver's side door, while shouting voices asked whether he was all right. He slowly sat back, and when he saw the blue glow of patrol car lights flashing strobe-like upon the snow, he knew that everything was in fact very far from all right.

Carlisle awoke from restless dreams and sat up abruptly, unsure at first where he was until the cold metal bunk beneath him where he'd slept in smoky clothes brought home the evening's nightmare.

There was one other person in the cell, a hulk of a man sprawled out motionless on the floor beneath him. The man would almost seem dead were he not snoring with such a roar that Carlisle pressed his hands to his ears. He sat that way for what seemed hours, watching with bemused disgust as a cockroach appeared through a crack and past his sleeping cellmate's face before disappearing beneath the cell door. This reminded Carlisle of something familiar. *What was it?* His lips twitched into a faint smile as he recalled his favorite old record—where in the liner notes Johnny Cash sees just such a roach in just such a place, and he envies its freedom. If only Carlisle could slip silently through a crack and disappear, too. But with that thought he heard the clang of a deadbolt, and the cell door swung outwards as an officer appeared and glared at him.

"How do you like your eggs? And sausage or bacon?"
Carlisle was startled. "Well, scrambled I guess. And I'll have the bacon."

The officer chuckled and thrust a plastic tray towards him.

"Here ya go boy, enjoy your breakfast." Carlisle took the tray and could hear the officer's muffled laughter even after he'd slammed the door shut and relocked it. The tray contained a small portion of mushy apple sauce and a slice of burnt toast.

The man on the floor had not moved, and his snores hadn't missed a beat while Carlisle sat back on his bunk and slurped a spoonful of applesauce. It was cold and bittersweet.

For some time he'd held his suspicions—though kept these to himself lest he appear a jealous fool if they proved unfounded, or (even worse) if he couldn't prove it one way or the other. Yet still there it was: His old friend Zack Terry always seemed a bit too keen toward Liz, Carlisle's wife of two years. And now that he thought about it, Zack had always appeared to over-indulge her. Ever playing the gentleman for one—what with his exaggerated motions of opening doors, pulling out chairs for her at bars, and always quick to light her cigarette.

He hadn't thought much about it at first. But now it occurred to Carlisle that Zack was even competing with him to impress his wife, so that Carlisle found himself almost unconsciously upping the ante. When the three of them approached a door together, Carlisle would attempt to sidestep his friend for the privilege of opening it first; when they approached a table, the two men vied to be first to seat Liz; and, though he didn't smoke, he took to keeping a lighter in his jacket pocket, fingering it anxiously until Liz reached for a cig when invariably the two men would draw like embattled gunslingers the moment it touched her lips.

To Carlisle's dismay, Liz visibly enjoyed these antics. She seemed to relish the sight of the two burly men scrambling around—as if fighting for a loose football—just to please her. (Both had after all been quarterbacks for South Carolina several years earlier, where they'd fiercely competed for the first-string position. Zack had won out in the end.) All the attention clearly turned her on—she even dubbed them affectionately "my two fightin' Gamecocks." For Carlisle, this all began to feel very disturbing, especially the way Liz began to react to his friend's attentions. He caught something in the way she would look at Zack at such moments that alarmed him, a sort of sidelong glance that lingered just an instant too long, her eyes slightly narrowing as she coyly smiled and brushed back her lush brown bangs.

Carlisle began to scrutinize his wife's face and movements whenever Zack was around. Especially unsettling was the manner with which she applied her lipstick whenever Zack addressed her. There seemed some hint of improper sensuality in the way she slid the tube across her lips. Hell, if it still made *him* erect, he could only imagine the effect this had on Zack.

Carlisle attempted to cut Zack out of their outings. And why was Zack always tagging along anyway? During the first year of their marriage, he and Liz felt sorry for Zack, whose own wife—also a college sweetheart like Liz was for Carlisle—dumped him for a married state senator. So Liz had set up a series of blind dates for Zack with several of her still-single Chi Omega sisters, though none stuck and one was an outright disaster: Barbara Ann Morris, a philosophy major now working on her Ph.D., who—upon feeling on her leg Zack's hand groping beneath the table—threw her glass of red wine in his face.

"Get away from me, you creepy fuckwad!" she'd shouted. She further suggested he return to whatever cave he'd come from.

After that the blind dates ended. But Zack somehow managed always to be with them whenever they went out. Even if Carlisle tried to avoid him, Zack would still seem to turn up wherever they went in the small town of Aiken.

"Hey! Mind if I join y'all?" he'd say, and then not hesitate to promptly do just that.

Most often this happened at The Polo Tavern, the late-night bar at the old 19TH century Hotel Aiken. There all the cigar-chomping Thoroughbred breeders partied during the Whiskey Road Foxhounds Hunt Week, the annual hunting festival held during the first week of February. One such evening, on an unusually cold night, Zack approached them and squeezed in between Carlisle and Liz at the bar. He seemed ecstatic.

"Y'all'l never guess what I just went and bought!"

Annoyed, Carlisle shook his head and gestured ambivalently. "I dunno, a horse maybe?"

"Horse *power* all right, come check it out!" They followed him outside where, parked right next to Carlisle's old pick-up, was a sleek vintage Harley.

"Holy shit!" Carlisle exclaimed, forgetting his resolve to appear to Liz ever disinterested in all things Zack. Bikes were a passion, however, that he could not hide. "Nice ride! Is that a '69?"

"It's a '67 dude! That bike's old as my old man!" Zack zipped up his leather flight jacket and flashed a toothy grin.

"Sweet! What'd it cost you?"

"Let's just say I pretty much put my life savings into this baby, but it's worth every penny."

Carlisle suddenly felt his stomach turn with envy as he looked anxiously at his wife. He knew how much she worshipped motorbikes, and this one happened to be her favorite color, too. Gamecock garnet. And now she was rubbing the tube of lipstick between her fingers even as she applied it, staring at the motorcycle as if it were a delicacy for which she had an insatiable craving. When she turned toward Zack, Carlisle saw that same expression transferred to him as she ran the lipstick around her fulsome lips.

"So when do I get my first ride, sugar?"

"How 'bout right now, baby!"

Carlisle hated it when she called Zack *sugar*. He'd always believed that marriage restricted even terms of endearment to the wedlocked couple. And why had Zack started out of the blue to address his wife as *baby*? Zack grinned at Carlisle sheepishly. Sheepish with a hint of wolf, Carlisle mused.

"You mind, Carl?"

Carlisle started to say yes, then hesitated. Along with a sharp jolt of jealousy that tied his stomach into knots, some masochistic impulse welled up at that same instant. And so he deliberately created the one scenario he most feared.

"Naw, y'all go ahead. I'll just hang out here and get another drink."

"Come on, baby!" Zack beckoned. Liz dropped her lipstick in her purse and turned back to Carlisle. "Here honey, watch my purse for me." She handed Carlisle the purse and as she walked towards the bike she shot him a backward glance. "I love you!" she called. Carlisle attempted a feeble nod and watched as Zack helped Liz onto the bike. She straddled the wide leather seat with her long thighs as if it were a horse. Zack started the engine and revved it up with such a throaty rumble that a group of people from the bar gathered at the door in a small crowd. Then Zack tore out of the parking lot with Liz clinging from behind, her long hair fanning out in the wind over her red fox fur coat. Carlisle felt something cold lightly brush his cheek. He looked up and saw that it had begun to snow, and remembered hearing a rare snowfall was forecast that evening.

One man he didn't recognize looked curiously at Carlisle as the bike rounded a corner and vanished down Whiskey Road. "Wasn't that your wife on the back of that bike?"

"Yeah, it was." Carlisle followed the crowd back inside and found a seat at the bar. The bartender looked at him.

"Jack and Coke. And make it a double."

The bartender nodded and set a glass on the counter and poured two generous measures of whiskey into it, followed by a quick spray of coke to top it up. Carlisle downed it and slammed the glass onto the bar in a not so subtle bid for a refill. He sat his wife's Prada purse on his lap and regarded it carefully for a moment. After a surreptitious glance around him to check if anyone were watching, he opened the purse and began to rummage through it. He unzipped a small pouch filled with credit card receipts, and there within found a slip of paper with Zack's number scrawled on it in his wife's handwriting. The gut-wrenching knot in his stomach tightened with a spasm that reminded him of the state fair roller-coaster, the time he was sure his safety-harness had failed and he'd be plummeting to his death at the next upside-down loop. He stared at the bar, where the line of polished oak metamorphosed into Whiskey Road, with Zack's bike cruising down it and Liz still gripping his waist from behind, her hair flying wildly as they veered right into Easy Street and to Zack's house on the corner.

He took out Liz's phone and attempted to access it, using the password she'd always used. It didn't work. He tried several more times just to be sure. She must have changed it! *And why would she do that?* He tried desperately to formulate every possible combination of every password his wife had ever used, but to no avail. He now had no doubt that her phone must be packed with illicit texts.

Carlisle's heart began to race. He now recalled every nuance that hinted of Liz's infidelity with his friend: every flirtatious gesture; each covert glance; the terms of endearment they'd traded right in front of his face. Deep down Carlisle had always suspected Zack, from the time they were roommates in college and he'd first introduced Liz to him.

He downed another drink and held out his empty glass. "Another one."

The bartender looked at him with concern. "I think you've had enough Carl. Want me to order you a cab?"

"No thanks Nick, I'm good."

"Sure man?"

"Yeah."

Carlisle put his best face on and managed to stand up straight, knocking over his barstool in the process. He grabbed his wife's purse, and looking over his shoulder he saw Nick watching him and calling a number on his phone. A few people laughed as Carlisle stumbled to the door grasping the purse. Outside, the snow was falling heavily now in large drifting flakes, the parking lot and tops of cars already painted white. The snow sparkled like clumps of diamonds in the light of dim streetlamps glinting through trees along the road.

Carlisle trudged through it carelessly. He dropped his keys and they sank in the snow. As he bent to find them he slipped and fell on his side.

"Fuck!"

He continued cussing as he frantically groped in a circle with his hands through the snow until finally striking his keys. They jingled as he got up and shook off the snow. Then he half stumbled and half slid to his truck. A moment earlier and he might have noticed the phone he'd left sitting on the dashboard light up with a new message; but instead he switched on the ignition and abruptly shifted to reverse, forgetting that his rear-wheel drive Ford pick-up was ill-suited for slick pavement. In his rearview mirror Carlisle could see the back of a parked suv quickly approaching. He hit the brakes and swerved right, only to feel himself sliding helplessly into the suv's taillights with a shattering thud.

He sat still for a moment trying to decide what to do now. But when he saw the bar door open and several people run out, Carlisle instinctively shifted into drive and careened left away from them and out of the parking lot onto Whiskey Road. There were few other cars on the snow-covered road, and he drove carefully in low gear for several miles until he saw the street sign at the intersection of Whiskey Road and Easy Street. On the corner was Zack's house, still in mid-February lit up with multi-colored Christmas lights that blinked at random intervals. They revealed a long white drive where, parked right at the end of it and covered with a custom fit tarp, he could just make out the silhouette of Zack's bike. And without thinking twice about it, Carlisle turned towards it, shifted into first and punched the gas pedal.

Zack's Christmas lights all suddenly lit up at once, and Carlisle had a moment of clarity. He slammed on the brakes and attempted to steer away from the driveway. But too late—the truck spun out of control and hurtled directly toward Zack's vintage Harley.

Carlisle had drifted off to sleep again when the cell door opened once more with a clang. The man on the floor twitched one foot and his snoring skipped a beat, but he remained otherwise unmoved as an officer looked in and motioned for Carlisle to follow him out of the cell. It was the same officer who'd brought breakfast earlier. Carlisle stepped over the sleeping man and out into a corridor lined with identical cells, each one occupied by orange-vested inmates. Some of them shouted at him and rattled the bars as he walked past. He felt a sharp pain and touched his ribs. They were sore and he wondered if the airbag impact might have broken something.

The officer led him to the station office. "We found this in your car boy, along with your purse." He smirked as he handed Carlisle his phone. "A little banged up but still oughta work. You get one call." The officer watched him as he powered up his phone. Its screen lit up with four text messages. They were all from Zack. He hastily scrolled through them, and the first was sent at 10:23 the evening before, long before Carlisle's midnight drive down Whiskey Road.

Text one: *Hey bro, it was getting pretty bad out there so I dropped Liz off @ ur place since its closer. She said u have a spare key hid outside.*

Text two (11:13 PM): *Hey man, just checking if u got home safe?? Please call! Hate for Liz 2 be stuck home alone. BTW she REALLY loves u dude!! All she talks about is how much she loves u.... Lucky guy!!!*

Text three (11:57 PM): *WHERE R U????*

Text four (12:44 AM): *WTF?!?!?!*

Carlisle pressed his hand to his cheek in a daze as if he'd just been slapped. He hesitated. Liz's phone was in the purse and the only other person he had in town to call was Zack.

Carlisle took a deep breath and dialed the number.

THE SAND OF SANTA MARIA

MADRID'S ATOCHA TRAIN STATION was engulfed by a flood of summer tourists, and it was to this chaos that I arrived, late, to catch the train to Seville. I pushed with my suitcase through the crowd of bewildered tourists standing in ticket lines and perspiring in the late morning heat. I already had my ticket, and looked on the information board to find from which track my train would be leaving. I was dismayed to see that it was to leave from track number twenty-three, at the far end of the station, and according to the huge wall clock, it should already have left.

When I finally reached the boarding platform, I was relieved to find the train still there with its last passengers climbing into its cars. The first whistle sounded just as I boarded a crowded car. I soon found my seat, put my bag on the rack overhead, and sat down by a window as I had requested at the travel agency. But I was annoyed that the only seats available when I bought my ticket were in the second-class smoking car, and so I would have to endure six hours of cigarette smoke. The seat next to me was still vacant, however, and I hoped it would remain that way so I could stretch out during the trip.

Another whistle sounded from the tracks, and I knew this must be the final call since we were already over twenty minutes late. Just then two people came quickly down the aisle toward the center of the car, where I sat. In front was a well-built man holding a bag in one hand and a train ticket in the other, which he compared to the numbers posted on the luggage rack above the seats. Following him was a young woman in a red sundress, and they both stopped next to me. The man pointed at the aisle seat to my right, and then lifted a bag into the overhead rack next to mine. He glanced at me quickly with a curious expression, but then turned and said something to the woman in Spanish. She suddenly broke into a laugh. The man embraced and kissed her, and she sat down next to me as he turned and walked away down the aisle. Almost immediately after he stepped down from the car to the loading platform, I felt the train release its brakes and slowly begin moving forward. Outside, the man was now visible through the window waving to the girl, and she waved back enthusiastically.

As the train moved slowly out of the terminal, red brick tenement houses came into view on both sides of the track, slums on the outskirts of the city. Above the shabby buildings, I could see the magnificence of downtown Madrid: the Palacio Royale with its golden spires, and the elegant villas across from Retiro Park with its tall pines in silhouette against the dark blue sky. Just outside the suburbs, the train began to gain speed, and from the window on my left I watched the tenements slowly disappear into bare fields that stretched away from Madrid. The city behind now seemed like a fertile island rising from a sea of baked earth. But soon the fields turned into wide grasslands, and in the distance rose dark lines of mountains. I had seen on a map that the trip to Seville would pass from the rocky region of New Castile in central Spain down through the La Mancha region, and on into Andalusia in the south.

There were no large cities on this route, but the train stopped at many of the numerous *pueblos* along the way. We only stopped briefly at these stations, but often in the midst of loading and unloading passengers a local peddler would board our car with a large pail of refreshments, moving through the aisle and shouting the names of his wares in lightning-quick succession:

"¡Hay cerveza—coca-cola—agua—limón!"

These peddlers were usually haggard gypsy men wearing ragged clothing. I bought a *cerveza* from one of them to save a trip to the dining car. I paid almost twice the regular price only to find the beer warm. By this time we were an hour outside Madrid. The car was very hot and many people were thirsty, so this particular peddler was doing good business. But he became so immersed in his sales he didn't hear the whistle blowing outside, and in the middle of a transaction the train started moving. Then he panicked, grabbed his pail and bounded for the back exit—too late. The train was already moving at quick speed, and he stood awkwardly in the back with a dumfounded look on his face. He looked even more helpless as he crouched down and leaned against the back panel, opened a beer from his pail, and gulped it down like a dehydrated fish.

I decided to drink my own beer quickly too since it was tepid and unpleasant, so I could follow it with a cold one at the dining car. I could also get some fresh air, away from the girl next to me who had been chain smoking since Madrid. She was reading a magazine, and had to move her legs so I could squeeze into the aisle.

Spanish *cerveza* was almost twice as strong as American beer, and soon after I returned to my seat it felt like a furnace had been lit inside my head. I began to feel a great intensity in all aspects of my surroundings: the clear murmur of passengers around me, and above all the steady pulse of the train's wheels like a cavalry troop galloping across the plain. The vibrations from the seat and floor ran through my body as if they were electric volts. Outside, the plains of La Mancha rolled by, green oceans of grass swaying under the bright blue afternoon sky. White windmills flashed in the middle of large fields, and occasionally we passed old Moorish fortresses crumbling from rocky hillsides. I pictured ancient battles between Moors and Catholics on the plains, their bloodstained blades glinting in the sun. I thought of the same scene centuries later, in the modern Civil War, when guns and bombs replaced swords and catapults. And I began to imagine those towering windmills transformed into evil giants besetting the hapless Don Quixote.

A noise from the back of the car caught my attention. A group of soldiers, all wearing the Andulasian emblem on their uniforms, were sitting together as a group, smoking and drinking since the train pulled out of Madrid. One of them was now singing, and soon the rest joined in with him. It sounded like a folk song from southern Spain, and as they sang they clapped in flamenco style—fingertips into palms in a syncopated rhythm. Everything felt exciting at once: the scenery, the rumble and vibration of the train, the singing and the rhythm of the clapping. I decided it was a good time for yet another beer, and tapped the girl next to me on the shoulder so she would once again move and let me into the aisle. When she looked up from her magazine and smiled, I noticed the way her wavy, light brown hair flowed seductively over the neck of her red sundress. And I realized then that she was beautiful. I wondered why I hadn't noticed this before. Then I remembered the man who had seen her off in Madrid, and my assumption that they must be lovers. But there was no reason to take that for granted. It was at any rate worth finding out.

"Do you speak English?" I asked. From her expression she was obviously surprised when I spoke.

"A little," she answered.

"Are you going to Seville?"

"No… I go to El Puerto de Santa Maria, on the coast in the south—where is Cádiz," she added, seeing my confusion. She spoke slowly, with a strong accent. Her name was Rosa, she said, though everyone knew her as "Charo." She was from Madrid and taking a short vacation alone for a few days on the coast. I asked indirectly about the man at the station; she replied that he was just an *amigo*.

"I'm going to the dining car," I said. "Would you like something? A *cerveza*, maybe?"

"Si… yes, that would be good." She moved her legs, which I now observed were tanned and shapely beneath her short skirt, and when I glanced back at her quickly from the aisle, she gave me a coy smile. In order to get to the dining car, I had to walk through several different passenger cars first, and one of these was the first class non-smoking car where I'd originally pleaded for a seat. It seemed excruciatingly dull and I was glad now to be in the second-class smoking car with its gypsies, singing, and the beautiful girl next to me.

When I got back to the seat with our beers, there were still around three hours before the train was due in Seville, and I talked with Charo as we rode further and further south. She was twenty-three, she said, and giggled to find I was four years her junior. The scenery outside the window gradually transformed into the dry, mountainous climate of Andalusia, and wide plantations dotted with olive trees rose and fell in slopes as we rolled by. The track followed the course of the Guadalquivir River, passing through Córdoba with its ancient mosque, and then beyond to Seville.

The conductor had only come through twice to check tickets during the whole trip. But on this second round, he discovered, hiding in the toilet, the gypsy peddler who seemed intent to stowaway until the train returned to his village later. The conductor was a large man of stout stature, and now he dragged the drunk and swearing man through the aisle, provoking shouts and clapping from the soldiers in the back. At the next stop, the gypsy was thrown off the train with his empty pail behind him.

When the train finally rolled into Seville, the day's fading light cast orange hues on the adobe walls of apartment buildings lining the track. Before the train rolled to a standstill, I suggested to Charo that we meet that night. (I was surprised to find myself so bold, but my natural inhibitions seemed to have been softened by the alcohol.) El Puerto de Santa Maria was about forty kilometers further south, and it seemed likely there would be a later train or bus there from Seville. The train came to a complete stop, and I stood up and took my bag down from the luggage rack. It is the custom in Spain to kiss those of the opposite gender twice, once on each cheek, at both meeting and parting. I wasn't about to break that tradition now, and I bent down to kiss Charo. But to my surprise she turned her face forward and kissed me directly on the lips. I felt a rush of excitement through my body as I took my bag and turned to hurry down the aisle and exit the train just moments before it departed.

I suddenly realized I'd not gotten Charo's number. But she had told me the name of her hotel, so I assumed I could easily find her. Now above all my earlier anticipation of arriving in

Seville, my thoughts were entirely consumed with the hope of meeting Charo that night.

Inside the station, I found there were no evening trains to Santa Maria. But I was only staying one night in Seville, and had planned to see the city the next day before taking the train back to Madrid in the same evening. (I was also on a very tight budget and could not afford to change plans and stay any longer.) My only hope now of seeing Charo again was that there might be a bus leaving to Santa Maria from Seville within the next few hours. Yet I had reservations at a hotel, and it was already past the check-in time. The travel agency had said all hotels would be full because of the tourist season, so to be safe I decided I'd secure my room first and then work on finding a bus for the expedition south. I got a taxi and gave the driver the name and address of the hotel. My mind was now so obsessed with meeting Charo later that, lost in this thought, I hardly noticed the sun setting over Seville in a collage of colors, or the stately palms that lined the city streets—nor the parks and gardens, where ancient fountains splashed streams of water into translucent pools.

After I checked in at the hotel and had my bag delivered to my room, I called another taxi to take me to the bus station. The driver asked if I was British, and when I said no, I was American, he became very jovial and expressed in English his love of American cars. Then I quickly explained my situation.

"But there is no bus to Santa Maria now," he said. I felt bewildered at this news, and the driver looked sympathetic. "I can take you to Santa Maria!" he said excitedly.

"In a taxi?"

"But of course! You can be there in, maybe, one hour. And it will not be very expensive," he added, observing my doubt.

The idea seemed absurd, but when I asked how much it

would cost, he said we could agree on a fare and then he would turn off the meter. He said he would be happy to do it simply for a change from the city; he only needed enough money in recompense to cover gas, plus a little extra to make up for the profits he'd be missing during his time away from Seville.

"Five thousand *pesetas*," he said.

Five thousand *pesetas*! That was too much. It was about fifty dollars, and that was all I'd brought from Madrid as spending money. I also had to pay for the room in Seville now that I was checked in, whether I stayed the night or not. I already had my return ticket to Madrid, but if I stayed in Santa Maria, I'd still have to get back to Seville the next day. I wasn't even sure if I could afford another room there at all—if things didn't go well with Charo romantically, I might wind up sleeping on the beach. I tried bargaining with the driver, explaining my predicament and offering three thousand *pesetas* instead. He seemed disappointed, but finally said he would take me for thirty-five hundred *pesetas*. We shook hands.

He switched off the meter and I found the number for Charo's hotel and called. She hadn't yet arrived, so I left a message with the concierge to tell her I'd be there around nine. It was now already eight. I nodded to the driver, and we left.

The last sunlight had disappeared as we rode out of Seville on a narrow two-lane highway, but the sky was clear and I could see bare moonlit slopes rising from fields on either side. The driver's name was Paco, and our conversation concerned flamenco and bullfighting—and American automobiles. At one place a huge black shape like a giant bull loomed up suddenly ahead of us by the road and I pointed in alarm. Paco only laughed and said to look closer, and soon the shape revealed itself in the headlight beams as a large billboard, in the shape of a fierce bull, advertising a popular *Brandy de Jerez*.

Finally, Paco said it wasn't much further, and I could tell from the landscape we were getting close to the ocean. After coming out of a range of hills the ground became very level, and soon Paco pointed joyfully to the darkness at right. We had reached the coast. Paco told me it was from the port of El Puerto de Santa Maria that Columbus had set off on his second voyage to the Americas. He said too that here was born the famous poet Rafael Alberti, who once wrote of how the sand of these beaches held the deepest powers of romance in all of Spain.

As we drove along the coast, we were both silent while the warm night air blew into my face from the open window with a roar like waves beating against a rocky shore. Watching the headlights penetrate the darkness ahead of us, I pictured Charo in her short red skirt greeting me with kisses. We would go to the bar for a cool drink, and then out for a walk on the beach where we'd be alone on the enchanted romantic sand as it sparkled under the starlit sky. Soon I would be kissing her, holding her tightly while the crashing waves drowned out all sound except the warm caressing breeze.

Just inside Santa Maria we came to a Stop sign. Paco pointed at it, annoyed.

"Stop!" he exclaimed. "Always stop, stop, stop. *Why* 'stop'? Here we speak Español!"

I refrained from comment, and, still grumbling, he asked the address of the hotel. This was a small town, and we were now driving down a long street lined with palms and rows of street lamps. But Paco seemed to be lost, mumbling to himself and peering restlessly in all directions before finally stopping someone walking on the sidewalk to ask for help. We found we were in fact quite close to the hotel, and soon Paco pulled up to its front entrance.

Then he said: "Four thousand *pesetas*!" This was five hundred *pesetas* more than we'd agreed. When I reminded Paco of this, he became enraged. I was trying to cheat him, he said. After all, he had to pay for the gas back to Seville, and he was missing hours of good business there besides. I saw there was no use debating, and paid his fare. He became at once very friendly again and held out his hand. I shook it with a resigned smile and wished him a good trip back to Seville. As he drove away, I walked towards the hotel entrance with just enough money to get back myself by train the next day. But I was thinking only of Charo.

When I entered the hotel lobby, I was surprised to find she was not waiting for me, and nor was she to be found at the bar. I stood there awkwardly for some time, waiting to see if she turned up. Finally, upon inquiry at the front desk, I received a message addressed to me. It was from Charo.

"I have gone away with *amigos* from town. Sorry to miss you. Charo."

I went out to the beach and walked alone over its mythical sand. Soon I sat down and rested against a sand dune, gazing across the bay where distant lights shone in the port of Cádiz. A wave rolled in along the shore as if reaching for some elusive desire, only to diminish and recede again, like a quenched flame, into the dark swirling water.

RING OF FIVE

Philby is driven by the incurable drug of deceit itself.
—John le Carré

There's no art to find the mind's construction in the face.
—Shakespeare, *Macbeth*

PART I

I

A MEDITERRANEAN BREEZE scented with gardenias drifted up to the balcony as Philby lit his pipe. The crescent moon glimmered through scattering clouds, and somewhere distant a seagull broke the humid silence with its wail.

Philby raised the pipe stem to his lips. As he inhaled, the tobacco burned with a crackle. The crimson glow momentarily lit up his face, revealing the rugged features of a middle-aged gentleman. A gentleman consumed with the gut-wrenching dread of what would come. The confrontation with Elliott that morning was wholly unexpected. And then there was the question of the note, tersely written in some obscure handwriting, which someone had slipped under his door earlier that evening. Was it authentic? Or was it merely a trap to test his resolve? He'd heard a shuffling sound outside his door, and then someone hastily descending the stairs. Philby had just missed catching a glimpse of the mysterious courier's face as he vanished in the shadows beyond view of the balcony.

Despite his misgivings, Philby abruptly tapped out his pipe, stood up and went inside. According to the note, he was due at the Port of Beirut in half an hour. He looked at the open, half-packed suitcase on his bed and shook his head with unaccustomed doubt. He turned and paused briefly in front of the mirror above the sink and splashed water on his face. If he'd had time to reflect, his weary and haggard appearance might have alarmed him. Indeed, his worn and fraying tweed jacket seemed to mock him. But now something else caught his attention—a barking dog on the street below.

He turned out the light and quickly moved to the window and peered through the curtains. A shadowy figure ran across the street. Then several more. As he looked closely, Philby could just make out the pattern of military fatigues. The police were surrounding the building! And one of them, standing in the light from an open doorway, a bulky square-jawed officer in a captain's uniform, was staring directly up at him.

Philby began emptying drawers and stuffing everything he could fit into the suitcase. Suddenly, he heard a loud shout in Lebanese, followed by the sound of boots shuffling into the building entrance and ascending the stairs leading to his flat.

He attempted to close the suitcase and spent a few precious seconds in a struggle to jam the over-packed thing shut, but to no avail. Then, hearing the footsteps approach the landing outside his door, he strode toward a small window opening onto an adjacent brick wall.

In the hallway outside, the square-jawed captain reached the top of the stairs. He led a group of soldiers to Philby's door and stopped. The captain knocked brusquely on the door, shouting in English with a thick Lebanese accent.

"Mister Philby?"

There was no answer, and the captain tried the doorknob. It was locked.

"Philby!"

With a nod from the captain, soldiers stepped up and kicked open the door. They burst into the room only to find it dark and empty, apart from the half-open suitcase still on the bed. The captain rushed to the balcony and saw his guards keeping watch below. Then he turned and saw the open window facing the brick wall. He looked out to find a narrow space between two buildings, with a ledge just a few feet above the window. He carefully climbed out, wary of the steep drop below the gap, and hoisted himself over the ledge just in time to see Philby disappear over the far edge of the rooftop.

When Philby landed in the grass below, he grasped his leg in pain. He bitterly realized he must have sprained his ankle in the jump. But the sound of sirens speeding toward the hotel steeled his nerves, and he hugged the ground on the dark side of the street as a police car sped by. Then he looked in every direction before hastening through the shadows, beginning a game of cat and mouse with his pursuers. It wasn't far to the port, and he had already plotted a course through the old cobblestone, labyrinthine streets leading from the waterfront.

He finally emerged from a dark alley to see the port and, beyond, the Mediterranean sparkling beneath the moon. The seascape was dotted with ships, but most prominent was the one now slowly docking ahead in the port. This was an immense grey freighter looming over the waterfront, and on its hull could just be made out the word *Dolmatova* painted in large Cyrillic script. Toward this ship Philby now limped determinedly, despite the increasing pain of his sprained ankle.

The ship was almost completely moored when he reached the waterfront, but just as he stopped at the water's edge, he heard a shout behind him. He knew enough Lebanese to understand the word *halt* and spun around to see a young guard, a few yards away, pointing a pistol at him. At the same moment a piercing whine of sirens announced the arrival of a convoy of military jeeps entering the port. As Philby stood facing the guard, the vehicles rounded the corner and came to a screeching stop. Moments later he found himself facing a wall of rifles, before looking once again directly into the eyes of the young officer who had first confronted him.

The square-jawed captain now stepped forward into the ring and approached Philby.

"You'll have to come with me, Mister Philby," he said.

Philby remained silent as he carefully regarded the captain. A shout in Russian came from the ship behind him, and the captain and his men all looked toward the freighter's deck at once. There they saw with alarm a long row of Kalashnikov rifles aimed directly at them.

Philby calmly dusted off his jacket, straightened up like a gentleman facing a firing squad, and nonchalantly ran his fingers through his hair as he finally answered the captain.

"That would appear extremely unlikely."

Philby stared penetratingly at the captain, who looked edgily from Philby to the stern cold faces of Russian snipers and back again to Philby. The young officer with the pistol watched both Philby and the captain nervously as Russian soldiers tossed ropes ashore to rig the moorings. In the distance a muezzin began chanting morning prayers from atop a minaret.

But the captain raised his pistol and stepped forward toward Philby. A shot rang out from above, and the captain fell at Philby's feet, a bullet wound straight through his forehead. Gunfire suddenly erupted from both sides, as the confused and now directionless Lebanese officers began shooting at random—helpless against the barrage of bullets showering down from the deck above. Philby glanced back toward the young guard just in time to see him ripped apart by a Russian machine gunner; then he dropped to the ground, his hands and face in a pool of blood as bullets whined above and men fell on both sides.

2

As Philby lay on the ground struggling to stay both conscious and alive, it seemed like ages ago since the things were set in motion that would lead to this moment, what almost certainly seemed to be the end of his life. Yet only fourteen years had passed since that lovely June afternoon in 1949, the day when he learned of Agent Blackwell's death.

He was at Trinity College, Cambridge, to celebrate his class reunion over an elegant dinner. The college Master had begun the proceedings with a black-tie reception in the college rose garden. Old friends mingled as a string quartet performed Vivaldi's "Spring." Philby uncorked a vintage bottle of champagne with a resounding pop and filled the glasses of the Master and two of his old college friends, Anthony Blunt and John Cairncross, before turning to others gathered around. Philby was in top form then and he knew it: suave, polished, witty, charming. But he also knew how to remain detached and ambiguous behind a seemingly warm and genuine personality.

The guests were suddenly startled when the college chapel bell began to toll. The Master drew out his pocket watch, clearly perplexed.

"A bit early for the bell, I should think," he commented. Philby lit his pipe with a knowing smile.

"More like a grand entrance, I suspect," he said.

"And need we guess who, I wonder?" commented Cairncross. The entourage then followed the Master as he paced toward the chapel and entered. At first their eyes had to adjust to the dim natural light filtering through the Baroque stained-glass windows. But what they then saw filled most with amusement and the Master with horror.

"Good lord!" he exclaimed.

Dangling there from the thick bell rope at the center of the chapel was Guy Burgess, swinging back and forth across the chancel and hollering like some surreal Tarzan while the swinging bell pulled him upwards and downwards in a circular motion. Adding to this spectacle was his flamboyant appearance, donning a foppish velvet suit and ill-tied scarlet bowtie. He looked like a perfect throwback to Oscar Wilde.

Standing nearby was Donald Maclean swigging from a bottle of champagne with one hand while occasionally giving Burgess a push with the other. He stood in marked contrast in appearance, appropriately dressed in a dinner jacket, and possessing the charm, grace and looks of a classic movie star. Upon seeing Philby, Maclean broke into a wide toothy smile and held up the bottle in toast.

"Hullo, Kim!" he shouted. Philby glanced back wryly at Blunt and Cairncross.

"Twenty years on, and you'd think they only just matriculated."

Later that evening they all gathered for a sumptuous candle-lit feast in the college hall, where long rows of crowded wooden tables led up to a dais at the end of the hall. The Master sat at the head of the High Table, where candlelight gleamed upon the antique sterling silverware. Nearest him, as guests of honor, sat Philby and Burgess. Next to them were Cairncross, Maclean, and Blunt.

The wine steward busily circled the table refilling glasses almost the moment they were empty. As soon as his glass was filled, Burgess downed his wine in one gulp and held out the glass for a quick refill. Now fortified with another full glass, he reached across the table and tapped Maclean's glass in toast with a wink. He rather inappropriately lit a cigarette, and then listened in to the conversation between the Master and Blunt.

"How is the King keeping these days?" asked the Master.

"Quite the royal bore," Blunt smugly replied.

Burgess took a thoughtful drag from his cigarette.

"Oh, Anthony," he commented. "Blunt as ever, I see! But I do believe congrats are in order for Maclean here."

"Is that so?" asked the Master.

"Certainly," Burgess replied. "He's just scored a posh posting with His Majesty's Diplomatic Service." They all looked curiously towards Maclean, quite tipsy after a full day's drinking.

"I've been appointed First Secretary at the embassy in Washington. Melinda and I are off to the States!"

"Excellent," said the Master, nodding with approval. And at that Burgess abruptly stood up and held out his glass in toast.

"Here's to Donald, Golden Boy of the Foreign Office. Reclaiming the Colonies for King and Country!"

"To Donald!" they all replied in unison. As he lifted his glass, Philby saw the old college porter at the far end of the hall, speaking to a server and looking anxiously in Philby's direction. He strode quickly toward the High Table and came directly up to Philby.

"Terribly sorry, sir, but..." The porter looked around nervously, and then whispered something to Philby, who nodded and stood.

"I'm afraid you'll have to excuse me. Good night." He turned and walked briskly away through the hall.

"Ah," said Cairncross, intrigued. "Hush-hush work, no doubt?"

It was late by the time Philby entered the Secret Intelligence Service headquarters at Broadway Buildings in London. The place was empty apart from the presence of C, pacing while waiting for his arrival. And on the desk in C's office was a half-empty bottle of Scotch and two glasses, which he proceeded to fill.

To Philby, Sir Stewart Menzies (known to all his minions merely as Chief, or—more fondly—'C'), once the formidable war leader of MI6, gave the impression of a gentleman who had become disillusioned with "the Game" of Cold War uncertainties. He was a man clearly weary of it all, burnt out and empty. A void he filled with alcohol. And scheming. But now

C looked genuinely worried, and he got straight to the point.

"We've had news," he said.

"Agent Blackwell?"

C's hand shook as he poured Philby another Scotch.

"I'm sorry. I know you were close." C raised his glass to Philby, who suddenly revealed a look of devastation as he stared into the glass silently before quickly knocking back the drink. C immediately refilled the glass and Philby finally responded.

"Intercepted?"

C looked down and nodded. "In Moscow."

3

Agent Blackwell, dressed in a dinner jacket, sat in a private box at the ornate Bolshoi Theater in Moscow, where a performance of *Swan Lake* was in progress. He raised a pair of opera glasses to his eyes, at first evidently enjoying the view of the ballerina playing Odette, the White Swan. Sitting next to Blackwell was Natasha, beautiful and sensual in a scarlet dress with matching shoes. She excused herself with a quick smile to Blackwell, and, as she moved past him, subtly brought her right hand over her heart and lightly tapped her chest two times.

Blackwell gradually shifted his view from the stage to the Tsar's Box at the rear center of the theatre, a grand spectacle overhung with red velvet curtains. There sat Stalin himself in his trademark Red Army uniform, an imposing figure with an austere face despite the moving performance below on stage. Blackwell now surveyed the various people around Stalin, until he suddenly found himself looking directly into a similar pair of glasses staring right back at him. He slowly lowered his glasses and the other man followed suit.

The man's gaze remained grimly fixed on him from across the theater. Blackwell knew, from the man's position immediately behind Stalin, he must be an elite KBG bodyguard.

The mood in the theatre suddenly darkened as the music transitioned to minor key for the climactic tension-filled moment with the Black Swan *pas de deux*. Blackwell stood up, politely excused himself to other spectators in the box, and quickly slipped out. The moment he entered the outer corridor, he began pacing rapidly through the hall without glancing back. A vendor at a table stocked with bottles of Russian champagne and caviar watched curiously as Blackwell strode past toward the fire exit.

When he reached the fire escape he began hastily to descend a precarious iron stairwell, only to see several black vehicles come hurtling around the corner below him. He attempted to retrace his steps, but looked up to see the stocky bodyguard from the theater appear above with a revolver.

Inside the theater, the tragic final moment of *Swan Lake* played out on stage and the audience, including Stalin, now with an empty seat behind him, stood as one in a rousing applause. But all Blackwell could hear of it outside was a muffled resonance, as he spotted a garden area just below and jumped. He landed in a soft bed of flowers covered in thick snow and made a quick recovery. Then he took off at a run away from the building just as the vehicles stopped and soldiers quickly jumped out to pursue him. He heard the bodyguard shout "Halt!" in Russian, followed by shots from the revolver as Blackwell disappeared into a narrow alley between blocks of apartment buildings.

He emerged to find himself looking straight out at Red Square. The specter of the Kremlin contrasted with the multi-colored dome of St. Basil's Cathedral, glowing in the light of the Kremlin towers' five Red Stars. He could see Red Army soldiers approaching from both sides now, and his only possible option was to run straight into Red Square. As he ran, he untied his bow tie and removed it. Then he took shelter behind a wall to catch his breath, and from an inner pocket sewn into the fabric behind the tie he slipped out a small packet. First he removed a slip of paper, which he crumpled into a tiny wad before popping it into his mouth and swallowing it. Seeing soldiers running directly towards him, he again took off running toward Red Square. With the grip around him tightening and escape clearly impossible, he slipped a small pill from the packet. Just as he raised it to his mouth, a shot rang out from behind and Blackwell was down, hit in the leg in the middle of Red Square.

When he hit the ground the pill flew from his palm and rolled out of his reach, and as he desperately tried to retrieve it with his outstretched arm he saw a black military boot stamp down on top of it, crushing the pill into muddy slush. Blackwell looked up to find himself encircled by a sea of Kalashnikovs. A hand reached down and picked up the crushed pill, and Blackwell raised his eyes to see General Viktor Abakumov staring down at him. Abakumov thrust the pill towards Blackwell's face. Then he spoke in English with a heavy Russian accent.

"Looking for this?"

Several hours later, Blackwell sat in a room completely bare apart from two chairs and a table, on which stood a bottle of vodka and two glasses. The table was surrounded by KGB counterintelligence SMERSH officers, including Stalin's bodyguard, whom Blackwell recognized from the Bolshoi. The only light came from a single bulb dangling on a wire from the ceiling, and Blackwell, stripped naked, sat facing Abakumov across the table—answering the same question for the umpteenth time.

"I've told you! I'm a bloody correspondent, for Christ's sake. I work for the *Times!*"

Abakumov appeared impressed that Blackwell could withstand hours of torture and yet still remain so defiant. He poured two shots of vodka and pushed a glass across the table.

"Drink, my friend! You need it. *Na zdoravia!*" Abakumov raised his glass toward Blackwell, downed the vodka and slammed his glass on the table. He seemed dismayed to see that Blackwell had left his glass untouched.

"As you wish."

Abakumov took out a dossier and laid out several documents on the table, including photographs of Blackwell and Natasha.

"Your name is William Blackwell. You are an agent with the British Secret Intelligence Service, sent to Moscow to record the movements of Comrade Stalin. On a mission no less than to plot assassination of the Great Leader himself!"

Abakumov leaned in close to Blackwell, scrutinizing him intently.

"This is the truth, yes?"

"It's rubbish," answered Blackwell. With a nod from Abakumov, Stalin's bodyguard struck Blackwell's head from behind, nearly knocking him from the chair. Abakumov continued.

"You have information we require. Information about this man." He held up a large photograph. It was a portrait of Kim Philby.

"What can you tell me of this gentleman?"

There was no answer, and Blackwell was again punched brutally from behind. Abakumov took out a sealed envelope from the dossier and pushed it over to Blackwell.

"Open it. It was found in your hotel room."

This time Blackwell complied, and with shaking hands he picked up the envelope, on the front of which was written in red ink the letters KP. He ripped open the envelope and drew out the letter. He slowly unfolded it, and suddenly looked startled. It was only a blank sheet of paper.

Abakumov abruptly stood up, then walked around the table and slapped Blackwell on the back.

"You seem to have drawn a blank, my friend."

Officers grabbed Blackwell and led him down a bleak corridor and into a small chamber, forcing him into a chair with his hands tied behind him. Abakumov stood in front of Blackwell with other officers behind. As Abakumov barked orders in Russian, Stalin's bodyguard pressed the barrel of a revolver against the back of Blackwell's head.

"Goodbye, Comrade Blackwell," said Abakumov, and then he looked up at the bodyguard before shouting the last word Blackwell would ever hear.

"Fire!"

4

C handed Philby a photograph from a dossier on his desk. "He was tortured and executed at the hands of this man: General Viktor Semyonovich Abakumov, Stalin's Minister of Soviet State Security."

"Bastards!" shouted Philby, in an uncharacteristic display of emotion.

"There's something else you should know," continued C, refilling their glasses as he spoke. "Blackwell was framed. And we think his mission got blown from a leak inside."

Philby looked up from the photo, perplexed. "*Inside?*"

"There appears to be a mole." C knocked back his drink. "But who, or where, is a complete mystery."

"Just let me get my hands on the bastard!" said Philby, knocking back his own drink. Then he paced to the window and stared out. He could see the Tower of London illuminated in the distance.

C looked at Philby thoughtfully. "That, my dear fellow, is precisely what we have in mind."

Philby spun quickly around, intrigued.

The next morning Philby arrived early at C's office. He'd spent a restless night, anxious to know what apparent promotion was on offer that C had promised to reveal in this morning's briefing. His wife, Aileen, was likewise keen to hear, and he had promised (rather prematurely, he now realized) to give her the details that evening.

When he entered the reception to C's office, the lovely Miss Pettigrew, C's secretary, greeted him with a smile.

"Good morning!" she said.

"Good morning, Miss Pettigrew. I believe C's expecting me."

"Yes, the Chief will be right with you. Do have a seat."

Philby smiled. "I always stand for beautiful ladies."

"Your mum taught you well then, didn't she?" answered Miss Pettigrew, flattered as always by Philby's attentions. She took out a cigarette, and Philby was quickly there with a light.

"Allow me," he said.

"Cheers," she said, lightly touching his hand as he lit her cigarette. At that moment a green light started to flash above C's door.

"It appears someone's giving me the green light," Philby said, with a droll glint in his eye. Then with a wink he entered C's office.

"Section Nine?" he exclaimed a few minutes later.

"We've decided to screen all personnel vital to state security," replied C. "To prevent any further possible betrayals to the Soviets. The PM wants to weed out all suspected communists."

"Can anyone ever really know another's true sympathies?" Philby asked rhetorically. But then more guarded: "What does this have to do with me?"

C took out two glasses and poured a round of Scotch. "How do you like it here, Philby? Do you find your work rewarding?"

"I do my best, sir."

"I mean, perhaps you find things a bit *too* quiet now in peacetime?"

Philby thoughtfully took a sip from his glass. He knew he must proceed carefully in his replies. One could never be entirely sure what subtext lurked beneath C's most innocent-seeming questions.

"On the contrary," answered Philby. "I joined the Service to combat Fascism, a war we seem largely now to have won. Apart from a few strongholds such as Spain."

"Quite right," C concurred.

"But I suspect," continued Philby, "that in the East things are on the verge of heating up more than most of us realize."

"Precisely! And that's what I like about you, Kim. You lack the complacency that seems to infect the lot of us here."

"Thank you, sir."

C regarded Philby curiously for a moment, then looked decisive. "We've therefore decided to form this new section devoted to anti-communist operations. They'll be entrusted with collecting intelligence about subversive activity in all parts of the world."

Philby frowned doubtfully. "Sounds like a very efficient use of our resources," he commented. "I thought our enemies were on the outside looking in, not the other way around?"

"You'd be surprised, my dear fellow. But we intend to pull out all the stops on this one. Our intelligence indicates things have gone from bad to worse. And then some."

"I see."

"And," continued C, with a reassuring smile, "in light of your exemplary service to us, I've recommended you to head this new section. You're the only man we've got who is utterly above reproach."

Despite his surprise at hearing this, Philby remained calmly staid. "I should be honored."

"Excellent! It's an ever more dangerous world, Kim, and we've certainly played our part in it. But now we must defend what is ours against those who would take it from us." C gestured toward a row of television screens along his office wall displaying news from around the world.

"Non-stop news on the telly," observed Philby, "and yet the public gets only a glimpse of the atrocious reality."

"Quite right, Kim. But the reality they see is more than sufficient. For our purposes, at least." C appeared to hesitate and reflect for a moment before pouring another round of Scotch. Philby looked curiously at a picture on the wall above C's desk depicting the ancient Chinese *yin yang* symbol of duality.

"I shall brief you more fully on your duties in due course," said C. "Have you any immediate questions?"

"Yes, actually. Has my appointment been cleared with MI5?"

"Just a formality, old boy," C answered with a reassuring smile. "Not even worth the bother. You're a Cambridge man, by God! And after all, I've recommended you personally as being the best we've got!"

"All the same," replied Philby, "for formality's sake, I should like to make it official. Would you mind getting a statement on paper that MI5 approve of my appointment?" Observing C's confused expression, he added: "I'd have that much more confidence in my job, having been officially vetted, you see."

C's face changed to a knowing look. "Ah, I see, transparency among the services. Yes, good thinking, Kim. I'll see that it gets done." He poured a further round of drinks and raised his glass.

"To Section Nine!"

Philby followed suit in toast. "Section Nine," he said.

That evening Philby returned home with Aileen from a concert in good spirits, laughing and affectionate as they moved quickly to the bedroom. Philby pulled Aileen into a warm embrace, but she gently backed away.

"Just a moment dear," she said coquettishly. "I want to show you something." Philby watched in admiration of her sensuous beauty as she gracefully slipped out of her dress and into a red, silk nightgown. "Like it?"

Philby smiled. "Mesmerizing." He again drew her into an embrace, and this time she consented. As he moved his hands along her back to slowly remove the gown, Aileen untied his bow tie and used its ends to pull him into a kiss.

"Do you think you'll get it then?" she suddenly asked.

"Get what … ? Oh, the job you mean? That depends."

"On what, may I ask?"

"On whether I get a clean bill of health from MI5."

Aileen unbuttoned Philby's shirt and caressed his bare chest. "And since when were MI5 concerned with health? But you'd better get this, love, I'm counting on you! Whatever it is…" She kissed him, then playfully continued: "But what, pray tell, could they ever have against you, Kim Philby?"

Philby returned her affection, kissing her passionately as they fell naked onto the bed. But she failed to notice the doubtful look that quickly passed over his face.

"Depends…"

5

The morning after their college reunion, Anthony Blunt stood in the lodge of Trinity College admiring the beauty of the centuries-old quadrangle, its manicured lawn sparkling with early morning dew. He'd remained in Cambridge for a few days enjoying the nostalgic remembrance of things past. This was a very special place for him; this is where it had all begun, which is what made the business at hand all that more appropriate. He was startled to hear the familiar old porter's voice behind him.

"Wish you were back in College do you, sir?"

"Hardly," replied Blunt, in typically pompous fashion. "This place always felt rather like being inside prison." He turned back toward the quad, where he observed Donald Maclean approaching.

"And whereabouts are you now, sir?" inquired the porter.

"For my sins, I work at Windsor."

"For your sins, sir," commented the porter, "you *should* be inside. Good morning, sir."

Blunt gave a wry smile as the porter disappeared back into the lodge, then greeted Maclean with a nod. Maclean appeared nervous. Blunt looked cautiously around before reaching into a pocket inside his jacket.

"You know what to do," he said.

Maclean nodded as Blunt pulled his hand from his pocket and slowly opened it. Maclean saw that in his palm was one half of a jigsaw piece depicting a five-pointed Kremlin Red Star. He quickly took it and slipped it into a pocket before glancing upwards toward a window. There, watching these proceedings from high above the quad, were John Cairncross and Guy Burgess.

Several days later Maclean arrived in Washington, DC, where he was welcomed as the new First Secretary with a formal reception at the British Embassy for him and his wife Melinda—a charming and polished young American woman from New York. They stood speaking with the British Ambassador, Sir Oliver Franks, next to a string quartet performing Vivaldi's "Summer." And they were soon joined by a middle-aged gentleman.

"There you are, James, I'd like you to meet our new First Secretary, Donald Maclean, and his wife Melinda. This is James Jesus Angleton."

Angleton shook Maclean's hand and then politely took Melinda's.

"Jim Angleton," he said warmly. "Welcome to Washington. I've heard great things about you."

"A pleasure," replied Maclean.

"As well as of course your lovely wife. Ma'am."

"Pleased to meet you," enjoined Melinda.

Angleton came across as a man possessed: At first impression, his folksy manner complemented a gentle smile and poetic sensitivity, but he also wielded a piercingly perceptive gaze behind his wide-rimmed glasses that could be unsettling to anyone with something to hide.

"Jim's a rare Yank indeed," said the ambassador. "Gentleman, CIA officer, and poet all rolled into one."

"And what do you do at CIA, may I ask?" inquired Maclean.

Angleton took on a serious expression. "You may ask, but if I told you, I'd have to kill you."

There was an awkward silence for a moment, and then Angleton suddenly laughed and playfully punched Maclean on the shoulder.

"Just kiddin' with ya!" he said. "CIA counter-intelligence. My job's to catch Commy rats. Whoever they may be, wherever they may lurk."

"Indeed," replied Maclean, somewhat shaken by Angleton's about-face.

"You'd be surprised how many of those nasty beasts are crawlin' around this great country of ours," Angleton explained. Then he gave Maclean an intense look masked with a cunning smile. "And we're gonna smoke 'em out, one by one," he continued. "It's a big country, but nobody can hide forever!"

6

MI5 Chief Dick White sat at his desk reading *The Times* over breakfast when his secretary slapped a folder down in front of him. It read: "MI5 Report on H.A.R. Philby. RE: Section Nine, SIS. MOST SECRET."

He picked up the folder and opened it as his secretary waited. The document inside simply read: "Kim Philby: Nothing Recorded Against." White promptly rubber stamped the paper with the MI5 insignia above the word "Approved." Then he handed it back to his secretary and sat back to resume his breakfast.

That evening Philby and Aileen sat with pints at a table by the fire in their local pub, The Markham Arms. Aileen raised her glass.

"Here's to you, darling, I knew you'd get it!"

Philby lifted his glass and tapped it against hers. "To *us*," he said. Aileen smiled doubtfully.

"But surely you can tell me for once what grand job you've got now?"

"Certainly dear," he replied. "It's a top job at the Foreign Office."

"The Foreign Office. Yes, that's obvious. But doing *what* exactly?"

"Just the sorts of things the Foreign Office *does* ... I really shouldn't bore you with the details."

"And why not?"

"Security." Philby winked at her. "Another pint? I'm off to the bar for last orders!"

"Ah yes, *security*. Cheers," she said, rolling her eyes in accustomed disbelief as she drained her pint. Philby got up and walked quickly to the bar.

The next morning Philby entered a small office at SIS headquarters, where he was greeted enthusiastically by a cheerful looking young man who immediately extended his hand.

"Nicholas Elliott, I presume?" asked Philby.

"My friends just call me Nick," Elliott replied as they shook hands. "I'll be assisting you as deputy in this section." Philby looked around at the tiny office and small staff.

"Are you sure I'm in the right place?"

"Certainly! Section Nine, right? Soviet counter-espionage."

"But I mean surely there's more to it than this? Stalin has an agency the size of the Kremlin."

Elliott appeared disappointed. "If you mean our rather humble exterior, keep in mind our budget's about as lean as a baked bean." He took Philby aside and added with quiet reassurance: "Don't worry, old chap. According to C, all this business about a leak has got the PM's ear now. I daresay we'll be the biggest outfit in the Service before..."

He was interrupted by the sudden appearance of C himself, who looked in and saw Philby.

"Ah, Philby, there you are. Tea at the Athenaeum. Sixteen hundred hours." With that he immediately vanished as quickly as he'd appeared.

"There you are then! I daresay you'll be getting an earful from C at the club!"

"Quite right. And knowing C, I suppose any tea itself shall be hard to come by."

When Philby arrived in the dimly lit smoking room of the Athenaeum Club, he found C sitting in a secluded corner at a small table between two ancient leather armchairs. C promptly handed Philby a Scotch.

"Odd blend of tea," commented Philby, taking a sip. "Something to celebrate?"

C opened a box of Turkish cigars and offered one to Philby. "How's your Turkish?" he asked.

Philby took a cigar and lit it. "Istanbul?"

"Precisely," answered C. "We're posting you there as SIS station chief. You'll be working out of the Consulate-General under diplomatic cover. Elliott will look after things on this end." C took a puff from his own cigar and watched Philby deliberate for a moment.

"Aileen and the children will be delighted, I'm sure," he said doubtfully. "But why Turkey, may I ask?"

"Main southern base for intelligence on the Soviets. Not to mention the entire Balkan region, and the ideal spot from which to launch operations."

"Operations?"

"We've decided to expand Section Nine to mount offensive operations. We need to penetrate communist bloc countries and carry out espionage missions."

The two men sat a few minutes in silence, as Philby considered the implications of this new assignment. Then C smiled reassuringly and stood up.

"How about continuing this discussion over a round of snooker, shall we?"

Minutes later, Philby and C were alone in the snooker room continuing their conversation over a massive, antique snooker table.

"And as head of anti-Soviet intelligence," explained C in mid-shot, "you'll be personally responsible for all our agents, both here and abroad. They shall report their intelligence directly to you."

"I've had very little experience in the field," Philby replied.

"Then here is your chance. But we see you as among the best we've got." C took a shot and just missed hitting the black ball. "Blast!" he exclaimed.

"That's seven to me, I'm afraid," said Philby, as he added seven points to his score.

"As *the* best we've got," continued C. "Consider it a promotion."

Philby now looked intrigued as he rapidly pocketed several balls in a row. Then he leaned toward C from across the table and asked with lowered voice: "Any leads on the mole?"

C's expression became serious. "The trail's gone cold. Dead cold.

We're counting on your expertise to blow his cover and limit damage. Key missions have been put on hold till we sort this out."

Philby made another shot as C added some advice. "So keep your ears to the ground in Istanbul, there's been increased activity along the Soviet border. Otherwise, I should hate to be a Russian expatriate at the moment."

Philby continued pacing around the table with confidence, speaking as he shot. "And why's that?"

"Remember General Abakumov?"

At this name Philby paused and looked up from the table angrily. "The man who killed Blackwell. Bloody bastard!" He powerfully smashed a ball into a far corner pocket and proceeded to clean up the table as C explained:

"Thanks to our little mole, Abakumov has acquired the names of Soviet dissidents abroad. Now he's dispatched an agent to Western Europe to assassinate them one by one." C paused to admire Philby's shooting. "Very impressive work, dear fellow, I must say."

By now Philby had reached the final black and hesitated. "Cheers. Any idea who they are?"

"The dissidents, you mean? Not an inkling … could be anyone from a list of hundreds. Anyone who's ever dared to criticize Stalin openly is fair game."

"I mean who is the agent?"

"Not a clue about that either. But he's probably at work even as we speak."

Philby aimed at the final black in a difficult angled shot. "The usual methods, I suspect," he commented. "Kill to impress." With that he potted the black in an impressive cross table shot to win the round.

"To impress, and to *warn*," added C. "Yes, I suspect so."

7

A pair of bright red boots advanced behind Vladimir Khromchenko as he stood on a London corner in Piccadilly Circus. He was waiting near the front of a queue boarding a double-decker bus.

As the boots neared him, a hand clothed in a ladies red leather glove slowly raised a folded umbrella, and then, with a barely audible *click*, a sharp spike popped out like a switchblade from the umbrella's tip. The hand raised the spike toward the back of Khromchenko's leg and stabbed him with a quick thrust.

"Ow!" shouted Khromchenko, spinning around with his hand on his leg. He raised his hand and saw blood, then looked around frantically only to see a puzzled old woman behind him and a blur of hats and umbrellas in the crowd.

He turned back upon hearing the bus driver exhorting him from behind. "Hurry up, please, you're holding up the queue. We haven't got all day!"

Khromchenko hesitantly climbed the steps into the bus and found an upper-level seat, squinting through the window to once more survey the street. Just as the bus began to move, he suddenly stood up from his seat, grabbed the support pole by the stairs, and started ringing the bell frantically.

The bus driver looked back in annoyance. "Hold your hat, mate! We're stoppin' at the next corner!"

Khromchenko began to choke and shake in violent convulsions, before letting go of the pole and tumbling down the stairs, landing on the floor beside the driver. Passengers screamed as the driver promptly hit the brakes and swerved over the corner as the bus skidded to a stop. Khromchenko lay dead, his eyes fixed in a deathly stare.

***

Late at night at the Atomic Energy Headquarters in Washington, DC, a cloaked figure with a flashlight prowled around a room. He rummaged through a file cabinet and hastily spread documents out on a table. The he took out his wallet and quickly turned it inside out to convert it into a camera. He proceeded to photograph the documents until his attention was diverted by the sound of approaching footsteps from the hall. He watched as the shadow of a pair of feet stopped outside the door and someone started working the doorknob.

The figure quickly gathered up the documents and hid in the shadows while reconverting the camera to a wallet and slipping it back into his pocket. The door opened and a security guard turned on the light and looked around curiously, then closed the door again and continued his rounds.

Meanwhile at the British Foreign Office in London, Guy Burgess sat at his desk over an early morning coffee, the perpetual cigarette in hand. Papers were strewn haphazardly across his desk as he stooped over it, writing at a frenetic pace while closely comparing various documents. On the television across from him, classical music played softly in the background as a BBC announcer introduced a special guest.

"...a rare tour of the Royal Art Gallery by the Surveyor of the King's Pictures, Mr. Anthony Blunt. Mr. Blunt, can you first of all give us a brief history of the collection?"

Burgess looked up with a smile at seeing his old friend on television, appearing staid and donnish as ever in tweed and spectacles as he stood in front of a grand portrait.

"Certainly," replied Blunt, "and happily we're standing next to the famous portrait of Charles the First by Van Dyke. Charles was one of the greatest collectors, indeed *the* greatest collector, among the whole line of English sovereigns. He founded the Royal Collection in sixteen twenty-five and…"

"Well done, Anthony!" exclaimed Burgess to himself, as he turned once again to his feverish work.

8

Light glinted from the tips of minarets silhouetted against the sunrise, as the dome of the Hagia Sophia mosque dominated the Istanbul skyline. High up on a balcony atop a minaret, a muezzin began to chant, calling the faithful to morning prayer.

From the garden of the Philbys' villa, the family admired the morning view of an ancient fortress on a bend of the Bosporus, with the dome of Hagia Sophia outlined in the distance. Philby's four young children, Josephine, John, Tom, and Miranda, played in the garden as the mournful wail of the muezzin continued to permeate the air. Philby pushed little Miranda in the swing as Aileen looked on.

The phone rang from the kitchen and Josephine ran inside to answer. A moment later she emerged again excitedly.

"It's for you, Daddy!"

Philby stopped the swing and gently lifted Miranda out and up into the air. "It's time for a rest, darling. And don't forget that if you swing too high, you might fly away and never come down!"

"But I *want* to fly away, daddy!" protested Miranda. Philby glanced at Aileen, and they shared a brief moment of tenderness. But within moments Philby had darted inside.

"Kim?" Aileen said softly, almost to herself. She looked through the window, and her smile transformed to doubt as she heard Philby's voice from inside.

"On my way," said Philby. He slowly hung up the phone, and as Aileen watched him she knew the charged intensity in his eyes could mean anything.

Philby entered an office in the British Consulate, high up with a sweeping view of Istanbul from the open window. Nicholas Elliott was there waiting, along with another man whom Philby didn't recognize. He was younger than Elliott, with— Philby mused recalling a phrase from Shakespeare—a "lean and hungry luck" beneath his wide-rimmed spectacles. Elliott quickly made the introductions.

"This is John Reed from the Embassy in Ankara, he'll be taking over for you here."

"A pleasure," said Reed, as he shook hands with Philby. Then, with a nod from Elliott, Reed exited the office leaving the two men alone. Elliott immediately opened a dossier, labeled "ATTN: Agent BFX-51, RE: MI6 Operation R5," and spread various documents out on the desk—some of them stamped "FBI: Top Secret" and "VENONA."

Elliott asked: "Are you familiar with Project Venona?"

"Only from a vague reference by C."

"Hardly surprising. The FBI keeps this so hush-hush not even the new American intelligence agency knows about it." Elliott hesitated a moment. Then he continued: "Hoover's convinced that Soviet agents have penetrated CIA."

"Typical Hoover," replied Philby. "But then how do we know about this? And what is it exactly?"

"I remember."

Angleton took another sip of sherry, and then assumed a more solemn air. "I wanted to give you a few words of advice, if I may, regarding your new posting . . . If, as a former student, I may make so bold?"

"But of course, my dear fellow! We're colleagues now, so fire away."

"I understand," resumed Angleton, "that you'll be liaising with the FBI as well as us."

"That is correct," Philby carefully replied.

"Now, FBI business is not generally our business, of course…"

"Of course."

"But you should know, if you don't already, that Hoover's not exactly pleased with your appointment."

"Oh dear, I'm heartbroken indeed!"

Angleton flashed a smile before resuming a decidedly serious expression. "He's very suspicious of British Secret Service activity here."

At this Philby angrily interrupted. "Not to mention, as I understand it, that of Catholics, Jews, blacks, liberals, homosexuals… Anyone, in fact, whom he considers *the other.*"

"…especially when it comes to joint CIA/MI6 operations."

"And your advice?"

Angleton deliberated a moment before answering. "My advice is simply to walk the fine line between pleasing one party without offending the other."

"Fair enough, but much easier said than done."

"This country seems to have one main agenda at the moment," concluded Angleton, "which certain senators have made a priority above all else."

Philby nodded with understanding. Angleton got up and prepared to leave, but as Philby helped him with his coat he added: "Oh, and be sure to take a careful look around your house."

Philby shot him a questioning look.

"The Russian A-bomb test took us *all* by surprise, and Hoover's goons are everywhere. They're seeing Red on every street corner!" Angleton exited Philby's office with a wink, leaving Philby alone and in deep reflection.

2

Even as Angleton spoke, on a dark London street corner splashed with rain, a pair of red boots exited a double-decker bus. Then a hand in a red ladies glove quickly opened an umbrella.

Minutes later Igor Gouzenko observed through his pint glass the same red boots approach the pub bar and a slim yet buxom figure slide into the bar seat next to him. In the next moment a graceful feminine hand, nails painted scarlet, held up an unlit cigarette to her lips.

Immediately, Gouzenko's hand was there with a light, which now revealed the woman's sensuous smile. It was Natasha, Agent Blackwell's sometime *femme fatale* from Moscow, but Gouzenko would never have guessed it from the thick cockney accent with which she now spoke.

"Cheers, mate!" she said, as she pursed her lips and blew a seductive ring of smoke directly into Gouzenko's face. "So whereabouts are ya from, anyway?"

Gouzenko replied in halting English. "I come … from Russia."

"From Russia!" she exclaimed. "Are you one of them commie bastards then, mate?"

"No!" Gouzenko replied in desperate earnestness. "I am no

longer Communist, I…"

"Well that's good then, isn't it?" interrupted Natasha, moving in closer and laying her hand flirtatiously on his thigh. "Because I don't suppose I could sleep with a bloody commie." She took out a tube of dark red lipstick and started to apply it, smiling at him.

Later that evening Natasha's umbrella stood propped up against a corner of Gouzenko's doorway as the sound of lovemaking filled his flat from the bedroom. There, Natasha was on top of him as they made love, and Gouzenko had the look of a man who had died and gone directly to heaven—a man who never imagined he could be so lucky and wondered if he were not now in some dream.

She reached behind her head and let her sumptuous blonde hair flow downwards over her breasts, and as she bent lower to kiss him, he felt the soft strands tickle the skin of his chest. Gouzenko suddenly felt overwhelmed at the image of her voluptuousness dominating him, and he lay back in anticipation of a triumphant climax. Natasha reached over to the bedside table and picked up the tube of lipstick; first she applied some to her lips, and then with a facetious smile she pressed it to Gouzenko's chest and drew a blood red line up from his belly to the space between his eyes as he laughed with delight.

He was just on the verge of climax when his laughter transformed into a gasp of horror. The lipstick pressed between his eyes vanished with a click and was replaced by a small gun barrel. He looked pleadingly into Natasha's deep blue eyes, which remained coldly fixed on his as she now spoke in Russian.

"Greetings from Comrade Stalin," she said. Then she fired a bullet directly through his skull.

3

Philby sat contentedly in a chair reading his British *Times* newspaper, sipping a cup of tea and puffing his pipe. Sitting there in his tweed jacket in a study lined with well-stocked bookshelves, he could easily be mistaken for a Cambridge don. Across from him, on the television console, a performance of *Swan Lake* was in progress, the music soft and soothing as he folded back the sports page and scanned the latest cricket results. He glanced through the window and smiled to see Aileen in the garden tending flowers with Miranda and Josephine, as John showed Tom how to kick an American football.

The light bulb in his reading lamp started to flicker and went out, and Philby put down the paper and reached inside the lamp attempting to jiggle the bulb. He stopped upon feeling something odd, then searched inside the lampshade where he discovered a small microphone sewn into the fabric.

"Bloody Hoover," he mumbled to himself.

Later that afternoon Philby sat in an office in front of a large desk, on which a nameplate prominently displayed the name "J. Edgar Hoover, Director." Philby watched as Hoover held up and scrutinized the microphone. Hoover appeared annoyed and took a thoughtful puff from a large Cuban cigar.

"I told them to come up with a smaller version of these things!"

"That isn't the point, sir...," objected Philby. "I..."

"Don't worry buddy, standard FBI policy," Hoover gruffly replied. "My motto is never to trust anyone until it's clear they're clean. Nothing against you personally, I assure you!"

"How long will my house be bugged then?"

"Three months tops, all being well."

"All being well?"

"We're on a state of alert here. The Ruskies just detonated

a bomb. Years ahead of when those liberal Commie fags at Central Incompetence said they would."

"But we're your closest ally!" protested Philby.

"Ally? How can you trust any nasty backstabbing foreigners when your own people can't be trusted?" Hoover got up and paced to the window, puffing his cigar as he looked out toward the Capitol building.

"According to Senator McCarthy, our government's infested with enemy spies. Hell, who's to say if even the President isn't stooping Stalin?"

"Indeed."

Hoover spun around and walked anxiously around the room as he continued.

"Communist party members, body and soul, are the property of the Party. And now they've stolen the most important secret ever known to mankind and delivered it to the Soviet Union. We've got a Red Bomb on our hands!" Hoover put his hand on Philby's shoulder. "The true enemy is the one which lurks within." He eyed Philby suspiciously and removed his hand. "Why do they call you Kim, anyway?"

"Kipling," Philby calmly replied. "I was born in India and my father named me after a character by Rudyard Kipling."

"Now what kind of a father would call his boy *Kim*? A boy named Kim!" he added sarcastically.

Philby attempted to conceal his anger. "My father is a great man. And if you'd bother to read the book, you should find that the character of Kim is a British agent."

Hoover finally returned to his desk and sat back in his chair. "You've lived up to your name then," he smirked. "Good to hear you're a *real* man, too, 'cause that's what we are in the FBI. Good grass roots beer-drinking men, unlike your Ivy League limp-dicks at CIA."

Philby listened to this tirade with stone-faced silence. He would rather have liked to get up and show Hoover how a real man throws a punch.

Yet Hoover pressed on: "Know what they teach those spooks at CIA, son? How to use knives and forks, how to marry rich wives!" Then he added, bluntly serious: "There just aren't enough real men with Intelligence."

"I couldn't agree more," Philby replied, suppressing a laugh.

"And we need every man we can get if we want to win this war," continued Hoover.

"What war is that, sir?"

"The war on Communism, of course!"

"Right."

"You see, *Kim*, this is a new kind of war. A war in which the enemy we fight is invisible, and might be anywhere among us lurking in the shadows. A war in which you're either with us, or against us." Hoover leaned forward across the table toward Philby. "Which is why you're here after all, to help us get to the bottom of the 'Homer' mole case." He opened a drawer and took out a document marked TOP SECRET and handed it to Philby. "Any of these names ring a bell?"

Philby quickly pored down a list of thirty-five names in alphabetical order as Hoover explained:

"Most of those names are low-level employees at the Embassy. I tend to suspect Homer will turn out to be a local recruit. A janitor maybe, or someone on the kitchen staff." He paused, and then smugly added: "Only a low-born would steal secrets for the Ruskies. I've got agents investigating every detail of every kitchen scullion's life. Along with his family and every friend he ever had or every girl he ever dated." Hoover noticed Philby's finger stop momentarily on the paper before continuing down the list. "Any thoughts?"

"Perhaps…" answered Philby, distracted.

"Keep in mind this is strictly between the FBI and MI6. CIA knows nothing about the 'Venona' decrypts and I intend to keep it that way."

"Understood, sir."

Hoover glared at Philby. "And I'm counting on you Brits to root out your little mole before he can do any more damage—to either of us!"

Philby nodded silently, before with a last look at the list handing the document back to Hoover and exiting the office with a sigh of relief.

4

Inside a steel reinforced vault in the Pentagon basement, a small group of officials sat gathered around a circular table in discussion. The flags adorning their nameplates revealed their nationalities as all being American, British or Canadian. Among them sat Donald Maclean.

At the head of the table and presiding over the proceeding was US Secretary of State George C. Marshall, a man of such commanding presence that Winston Churchill once dubbed him "the noblest Roman of them all."

"The President," he began, "has authorized these talks on countering the solid Communist bloc formed by the Soviet Union. Moscow has now destroyed the independence and democratic character of a whole series of nations in Eastern and Central Europe. We may well be on the verge of World War III, a war of destruction to threaten humanity itself." He pointed at a map of Europe and continued: "President Truman has asked the Joint Chiefs of Staff to produce an emergency war plan for Europe. We are, therefore, proposing a North American-Western military alliance. Such an alliance will serve as a united front against Communism, and a bastion of hope and freedom for Western Europe and the world."

Marshall paused and stared gravely at the assembly. "Let me remind you, gentlemen, that in the interest of security there will be no note-taking whatsoever during these discussions. The State Department can take no chances on allowing information of US war plans to leak to the Soviets. Nothing said here is ever, and I repeat *ever*, to leave this room."

Later that night a figure with a briefcase appeared in silhouette at the top of a Washington alley, lit only by the light of a street lamp feebly permeating a fine mist. He cast a long shadow against the light, and behind him at a distance rose the dimly illuminated Washington Monument. When he entered the alley, another figure in a dark overcoat and hat emerged from the shadows. As the two approached each other, the first took something from his pocket and held it out. The other followed suit, and after a moment two jigsaw pieces were fitted neatly together to form a Kremlin Red Star.

The second figure took out a cigarette and lit a match, and in the flickering light Maclean's eyes shone nervously as he removed a file of documents from the briefcase and handed it over. The other man stuffed the file beneath his overcoat and, without a word, vanished again down the alley as Maclean turned and strode swiftly away in the opposite direction. Maclean, still shaking, entered a nearby bar he knew only too well. Everyone there seemed captivated by someone making a speech on television. Maclean sat at a barstool and watched as Senator Joseph McCarthy addressed the State Department:

"...for this is not a period of peace. This is a time of the Cold War. This is a time when the world is split into two vast, increasingly hostile armed camps—a time of a great armaments race. Today we can almost physically hear the mutterings and rumblings of an invigorated god of war. You can see it, feel it..."

Maclean signaled the bartender. "Double Scotch on the rocks, please." As the bartender prepared his drink, Maclean looked curiously at the television and lit a cigarette.

"...hear it all the way from the hills of Indochina, from the shores of Formosa right over into the very heart of Europe itself. Today we are engaged in a final, all-out battle between communistic atheism and Christianity..."

The bartender handed Maclean his drink. "Cheers," he said, taking a quick drink while continuing to watch McCarthy's speech.

"The reason why we find ourselves in a position of impotency is not because our only powerful, potential enemy has sent men to invade our shores, but rather because of the traitorous actions of those who have been treated so well by this nation. It has not been the less fortunate or members of the minority groups who have been selling this nation out, but rather those who have had all the benefits that the wealthiest nation on earth has had to offer—the finest homes, the finest college education, and the finest jobs in government we can give. This is glaringly true in the State Department. There the bright

young men who are born with silver spoons in their mouths are the ones who have been the worst."

Maclean laughed to himself, then smiled at the bartender as he gestured toward the television. "What a nutter!"

The bartender regarded Maclean suspiciously. "Why do you say that? I think he makes a lot of sense! Where are you from anyway? You sure don't sound American, buddy."

Maclean ignored him and finished his drink in one gulp and slammed down his glass. The bartender grudgingly poured another as Maclean looked back at McCarthy, now displaying a piece of paper he held in his outstretched hand.

"I have in my hand fifty-seven cases of individuals who would appear to be either card-carrying members or certainly loyal to the Communist party, but who nevertheless are still helping to shape our foreign policy. One thing to remember in discussing the Communists in our government is that we are not dealing with spies who get thirty pieces of silver to steal the blueprints of new weapons. We are dealing with a far more sinister type of activity because it permits the enemy to guide and shape our policy..."

Maclean polished off his Scotch, slapped money on the bar and abruptly stormed across the room towards the door.

"Fascists!" shouted Maclean as he departed. But unobserved to him was a figure sitting alone and watching this spectacle in silent interest. Had Maclean been more attentive, he might have taken note of the presence of James Jesus Angleton.

Melinda lay asleep on the couch when Maclean finally arrived home. An empty wine bottle stood next to her on the coffee table, and the flickering TV illuminated her pale face with a ghostly glow. She opened her eyes at the sound of screeching tires outside and abruptly sat up as headlights shone through the curtains. Moments later she heard someone fumbling with keys outside the door before it opened, and when Maclean entered and stared at her with bleary-eyed surprise, Melinda glared back at him.

"Where have you been?" she demanded.

Maclean said nothing as he carefully hung up his hat and coat.

"Couldn't you have called, for Christ's sake?"

"I had work to do."

"Work?" She was shouting now, then sniffed suspiciously. "You call coming in at all hours of the morning reeking of whiskey *work?*"

Maclean tried to embrace her, but she backed quickly away. "Come on, darling," he pleaded, "let's not have another row over this." He looked at her dejectedly as she started to cry.

"Don't 'darling' me, Donald! I don't know what you're doing, and I don't think I really want to know. But sometimes I think I don't even know my own husband anymore. Ever since we moved to Washington."

"I have some good news then!"

Melinda turned back around, a curious expression now on her face. Maclean attempted a feeble smile. "You've been saying you'd like a change of scenery. Well, you shall have one!"

She looked at him questioningly. "Where?"

"I'm being posted to Cairo."

"Cairo?"

She sounded incredulous, and now Maclean tried to make the best of what he knew to be an impossible situation.

"Yes, Cairo! You've always said you wanted to see the pyramids at Giza."

"See them, not move into them! What about my family in New York? That's where I wanted us to move."

"Bloody hell! There's no pleasing you, is there?"

"Not when all you do is treat me like some sort of trophy. You only take me out when there's some fancy reception, where I can ornament your arm."

"Melinda…"

"The posh Brit diplomat's charming Yank wife, who spends the rest of her time stuck at home while her husband's out God knows where."

"Melinda," Maclean said again, attempting to embrace her. She pushed him forcibly away.

"Fuck you!" she shouted, then threw herself on the couch and started to weep. Maclean sat next to her and this time she allowed him to comfort her.

"I just want a normal life, that's all," she said. "Like we used to have."

"We will, darling. After the Cairo posting's up, we'll move to New York."

She looked at him doubtfully, still crying. "Promise? You must promise me this time Donald, and not just get my hopes up falsely again."

"Promise," he said, and she finally embraced him. But she couldn't see the look of doubt on the face he wore over her shoulder.

"When do we go?"

"Soon as my tour here expires. Early summer. And you'll never guess whom they've chosen as my replacement at the embassy!"

They looked at each other a moment in thoughtful silence, suddenly broken by the sound of a baby crying in the bedroom. Melinda got up.

"And who's that?"

"My best mate from Cambridge!" Maclean said enthusiastically. "Guy Burgess."

5

Philby and Angleton sat at a table at Harvey's Restaurant as waiters arrived with two massive lobsters.

"Good god, Jim!" exclaimed Philby. "You say you do this weekly? And yet you're still as thin as a broomstick, old chap!"

"The benefit of hard work, my friend," Angleton replied. "And gardening."

"Gardening?"

Angleton dug into his lobster voraciously like a man famished. Philby seemed something at a loss with his own.

"Wild orchids take a lotta work," Angleton resumed, a subtle smile forming on his lips. "Especially when the garden's dug up with moles. In fact," he added, finishing a particularly large bite of lobster, "I caught one just the other day." He dabbed his mouth with his lobster bib and looked up at Philby with a smile.

"Then perhaps you should try poison," answered Philby, carefully playing along.

"I did. But you know, oddly enough the bastards have gotten so clever that the moment you've tried one thing, the others pick up on it just like that." Angleton snapped his fingers. "And dig in even deeper."

Philby refilled Angleton's wine glass before topping up his own. "Then I suppose you'll just have to dig more deeply yourself."

"Oh, I have, I assure you. And you know what's funny? I'm starting to think it's a kind of conspiracy." Angleton chuckled as Philby remained silent. "A conspiracy of moles! And I'd bet anything it's not just my garden that's affected. I'll bet they're everywhere, all over Washington!"

"Indeed."

Angleton cracked open his lobster tail; Philby observed curiously and attempted to follow suit with his own. "Yes indeed, and I'd suggest you look carefully at your own garden. Let one mole have its way, and you're finished."

"I shall bear that in mind," Philby said, watching warily as Angleton now leaned forward at him over the table with a most penetrating gaze.

"And I'll tell you a little secret, Kim. I was just over at the British Embassy the other day, and by the looks of their garden I'd say you've got a mole there for sure." Philby smiled as he finally managed to open his lobster tail with an ear-splitting crack.

Later that afternoon, Angleton and Philby sat in the office of CIA Deputy Director Allen Dulles, who contentedly puffed a large pipe as he debriefed them from behind a broad oak desk.

"...and in the global war on Communism, we can miss no opportunity to subvert the enemy on his own territory. Because what's at stake here is the one thing this country..." Dulles cleared his throat. "*Our* countries hold most dear: Freedom. We, gentlemen, are the vanguard on the frontline of this new Cold War. Conventional troops are just for show. The real battles are fought by us beneath the surface, beyond the ken of both the media and the people. Even our leaders are often in the dark about our work." Dulles handed each man a dossier, which they began to thumb through as he continued. "Our respective governments have sanctioned a covert operation in Eastern Europe. We wish to splinter a Soviet bloc country from Moscow's control."

"Albania," observed Philby, reading through the dossier.

"Albania. The smallest and weakest of the Socialist states, with northern and eastern frontiers bordering Yugoslavia. And bounded on the south by Greece, a Western ally with which Albania is still technically at war. The State Department and

British Foreign Office want CIA and SIS to execute this operation. And as colleagues in counter-intelligence, I'm placing the two of you in joint command." Dulles smiled. "Nice to know you're old friends from our OSS days in London."

"Where will operations be HQ'd?" Angleton enquired.

"The Greek island of Corfu. Three miles from the Albanian coast. Your mission is to infiltrate teams of anti-Communist Albanian exiles past the border. We've provided them with guns, radios and explosives. They've been trained to provoke counter-revolution in the country. With luck, civil war will topple the regime in Tirana and ignite anti-Communist uprisings throughout the region. And the Soviet Empire will crumble from the seams. It's all in the dossier. Any further questions?"

Angleton and Philby exchanged a quick glance.

"Then I suggest you start packing!"

The two men closed their dossiers and rose together with a nod to Dulles.

Three days later Philby stood with Angleton on a sun-drenched boardwalk in Corfu. Philby surveyed with pleasure the rows of white stucco houses rising from the harbor above the sapphire-blue water.

They walked onto a landing where Angleton led Philby toward what appeared to be an old fishing boat that had seen better days. A fisherman holding a rod, its line dangling over the dock, stood up and blocked their way.

"How's the fishing?" asked Angleton nonchalantly.

"Not so good, only caught one redfish so far."

"Maybe you should try a new angle."

"Good idea." With that the fisherman reeled in his line,

which, Philby observed, contained but a bare, baitless hook. He motioned the men to enter the boat, and as they walked past he recast his barren line into the water.

Angleton led Philby into a cabin. To Philby's surprise it was full of sophisticated communications equipment. Several CIA operatives busily spoke into radios as messages clicked through on a telegraph. They hardly seemed to notice the new arrivals.

"Very impressive," said Philby.

Angleton smiled. "Part of our nexus of CIA Balkan operations."

A young radio operator fighting against static looked up at Angleton. "Rendezvous with Operation Icarus personnel at nineteen hundred hours, sir."

By sunset Philby and Angleton stood on the beach observing a huge celebration. Groups of young Albanians sang and danced around a bonfire, upbeat about their mission.

"They're good to go at midnight," said Angleton.

Philby nodded, and at that moment a young man with a guitar and a hauntingly plaintive voice began singing an Albanian folk song. Others joined in and began to dance. As Philby watched and listened, deep in thought, a beautiful young woman left the group and came up to him and took his hand, pulling him into the circle of dancing revelers. As he awkwardly attempted to imitate her intricate, rhythmic movements, she laughed good-naturedly with a voice that seemed to Philby like some ethereal, enchanted music. He laughed in turn, but the smile he flashed was bittersweet.

"And what is your name, may I ask?"

"My name? Anastasia. My English is not so good."

Philby looked into her dark brown eyes. The hopeful innocence in her expression suddenly moved him deeply. He looked up towards Angleton and nodded. In the flicker of firelight that played on Philby's face, Angleton discerned an unsettling look of resigned sadness.

At midnight the two men and their operatives watched as a small boat made its way quietly through the darkness across the bay. Philby could see among the Albanian exiles Anastasia sitting next to the young guitarist. They held hands as they peered nervously ahead toward the distant shore of their homeland—where, just visible through the fog-enshrouded shore, a flashing beacon signaled to them from the Albanian coast.

An hour later Philby, Angleton and the CIA operatives all stood anxiously by the radio as the operator adjusted the dial, trying to find the right frequency.

"Icarus to Saturn, over… Icarus to Saturn…"

Behind them the telegraph began clicking busily with an incoming message. The radio operator glanced quickly over it. When he saw that it began "ATTN: Philby" he started to speak, but a faint voice now crackling from the radio cut him off as everyone listened intently.

"*Contact … with loyalists … welcomed … all ok … safe to send other groups … soon as possible … I repeat … safe … send others as soon as possible.*"

At this the operatives all cheered at once. Philby held out his hand to Angleton.

"Well done, dear fellow. You're progressing nicely. I daresay I shall be learning from you before too long."

Angleton grinned. "I'll bet you still have a few tricks up your sleeve you didn't teach us in London." At that moment the radio operator hurried up to Philby. "Message for you, sir. From Istanbul."

"Istanbul…" muttered Philby, glancing over the message. And his face suddenly soured.

***

Philby found himself two days later back in Istanbul, where he sat in John Reed's office at the British consulate.

"And how's my replacement handling Istanbul?"

"Surviving. Just don't ever make the mistake of calling this place *Constantinople* as I once did soon after arriving. I thought they were going to plunge a spit up my arse and make a shish kebab of me!"

Philby chuckled. "Likewise never tell a Greek you're going to *Istanbul*." Reed picked up a photograph from his desk and handed it to Philby.

"Konstantin Volkov, my opposite number here at the Soviet Consulate. He paid me a midnight visit the other night. He's requesting asylum in Britain for himself and his wife."

Philby raised an eyebrow in surprise. "Is he offering anything in return?"

"He is indeed. And that's why C wants you to handle this case personally. It appears Volkov does more than just run the Consulate."

"Fancy that."

Reed smiled. "He's also a KGB officer, and is offering details of Soviet counter-espionage operations."

"What sort of details?"

"He's promised to reveal Intelligence of Soviet networks and agents operating abroad. Including the real names of seven Soviet agents working undercover in British agencies."

Philby took a deep breath. "Any specifics?"

"Apparently, two of them are with the Foreign Office. And another is an officer in the Secret Intelligence Service itself."

Philby stared at the photograph. "R5," he said thoughtfully to himself.

"Sir?"

"I think we're on to something of the greatest potential importance here, John. But we need to confirm the authenticity of his information, as he could be just a Soviet plant. I'd like a little more time to look into this before recommending action."

That night Philby sat at a desk in front of a window looking out toward the Hagia Sophia mosque, its minarets lit up in the night like beacons. As he contemplated Volkov's photograph, he filed through the original 'R5' and 'Homer' documents Elliott had given him before he left Istanbul for Washington. Then Philby picked up the phone.

When Philby arrived at Reed's office the next morning, Reed picked up the receiver from his desk phone and dialed a number.

"I often have routine consular business with Volkov," Reed explained. "So it'll seem perfectly normal to invite him over to talk."

Reed pushed a button to activate the speakerphone, and a woman's voice answered from the other end.

"Dovray otra, da?"

"Good morning, this is John Reed from the British Consulate. I'd like to speak with Konstantin Volkov, please."

Reed smiled at Philby reassuringly. Then a loud and gruff male voice came through the speaker.

"Da?"

Reed appeared surprised. "Good morning, I wanted to speak with Konstantin Volkov."

"This is Volkov," replied the voice. "How may I help you?"

"I think there's some mistake here," said Reed. "I wish to speak with *Konstantin* Volkov, the First Secretary."

"I am Volkov," repeated the voice. "How may I help you?"

Reed looked doubtfully at the receiver in his hand; then they heard a *click* from the other end as the phone was hung up.

Philby stared at Reed. "What seems to be the problem?"

"That's *not* Volkov, I know his voice perfectly well!" Reed dialed again, and again the female receptionist answered.

"*Da?*"

"Yes," Reed persisted, "I'm trying to reach *Konstantin Volkov*, the First Secretary."

"I'm sorry," came the reply, "but Volkov is in Moscow."

There came through the speaker the sound of a scuffle and a door slamming, and then with another sharp CLICK the line went dead. Reed appeared flabbergasted.

"And just a minute ago she put me on with him! Whoever *he* was."

Reed and Philby drove to the Soviet Consulate, where Reed angrily confronted the receptionist: "I demand to speak with Konstantin Volkov!"

"Who?"

"Volkov. The First Secretary."

"There is nobody here by that name."

"What?"

The receptionist looked across the room toward a gruff looking official observing them.

"Volkov?" she asked.

The official shook his head no. Reed shrugged in exasperation as he looked back at Philby.

"What a bloody madhouse!"

That afternoon a Soviet military aircraft suddenly landed without clearance at the Istanbul airport, taking air traffic controllers by surprise. They watched with further disbelief as a car raced out to the tarmac, where several Soviet officials loaded a heavily bandaged figure from the car onto a stretcher and lifted it onto the plane.

The aircraft immediately took off and vanished into the Eastern horizon.

PART III

I

When Philby returned to Washington, he found a stack of letters waiting on the desk in his study. As he flipped through them one letter stood out. It bore simply the letters "KP" in red ink over Philby's address. He opened it and smiled to see the letterhead: GUY BURGESS. The letter was quick and to the point.

DEAR KIM,

Prepare yourself for a shock. I have been posted to Washington to replace Maclean at the embassy, effective early summer, and should be truly grateful for any hospitality you might offer upon my arrival.

As ever,
—GUY

Philby walked out into the garden, where he found Aileen busy weeding with a hoe while the children played in the yard behind her. She looked up as Philby strode towards her.

"Good news darling!" he said excitedly, holding up the letter. "Remember my old friend Guy, from college?"

Aileen frowned. "Do you mean that piss-head ponce who went berserk at our wedding reception, when daddy had to call the coppers to haul him away?"

"Oh dear, I'd forgotten about that. One of his less-dignified moments, I'll admit. But yes, that's the one I mean."

"Then I suppose I do remember him, and all too well!" Aileen looked at her husband suspiciously. "So what's this good news then?"

Philby hesitated. "Well, I just got a letter from Guy saying the Foreign Office is sending him here to Washington."

Aileen stared at him incredulously. "Him? But he has a pathological hatred of America!"

"All the same, he's hoping I … *we* can put him up for a while, just until he gets settled in."

"And I do hope you'll inform him how impossible that is?"

Philby became defensive. "Not at all! I think it would be great fun. Besides, I owe him."

"Fun for you, perhaps," Aileen interrupted. "But I will *not* have that obscene drunkard prancing round our house." She gestured frantically towards the children. "What about them?" The children had stopped their play to observe their parents' argument.

"They'll be fine. No, I've made up my mind. I shall tell Guy that he's welcome to stay with us."

"But…"

"He'll be here in June, so you've got plenty of time to prepare."

Philby turned to walk back, but Aileen called to him pleadingly. "You know good and well he'll never leave our house once he's here!"

But Philby turned his back to her again and walked away into the house, slamming the door after him. Aileen grabbed her hoe and swung it furiously into a patch of weeds.

Later that morning Philby was summoned to the British Embassy. The ambassador had called in person, saying the news was urgent. When Philby arrived he found the ambassador in his office speaking quietly with another man whose back was turned to the door. But when he turned around, Philby was taken aback. It was C and his look was grave.

"Chief!"

C got straight to the point. "I'm afraid I have some very bad news. Do have a seat, Philby." Philby complied and looked at C questioningly.

"We lost them all," said C. "Every last one of them."

"Who?"

The ambassador stifled a cough. "The Albanian mission was an unqualified disaster," he said. Philby suddenly looked distraught.

"But how? When we left, everything was going smoothly. The radio communication that came back was all positive."

C glanced at the ambassador, and then back to Philby. "So it seemed. In actuality, it was all an elaborate ruse. After the initial contact, all communication ceased. This in itself wasn't necessarily of concern, but after a month without contact we began to worry."

The three men sat in silence for a moment. Philby could sense what was coming.

"There was one survivor," continued C. "He finally made it back to Greece and said that every team had been wiped out immediately upon landing."

Philby abruptly dropped his head into his hands. "Dear God…" He looked back up at C, his eyes reddening in disbelief. "And the radio communications?"

"They were playing a cruel game," explained the ambassador.

"Somehow the Albanian security service penetrated our operation and placed an agent among the insurgents."

C nodded in agreement. "And once the first group had landed and were captured, Albanian security forced the radio operator to lure the rest of the teams to follow." Philby appeared devastated, but remained silent as C stared at him thoughtfully.

"I suppose I don't need to tell you what all this means?"

Philby nodded. "R5. If only I'd found the bastards in time!"

C stood and paced the room. "Yes, and the spy ring is clearly able to penetrate our deepest security measures. We simply *cannot* allow it to continue. Every agent we send into the field is in danger. American as well as British, which severely compromises the future of sis/cia cooperation, especially if cia discovers a British mole is at fault!"

"Which it will," concurred the ambassador, "if we don't find him first."

"Much less suspect he's not alone," added C. "So be very careful Philby in your dealings with Deputy Director Dulles. It's clear now that R5 has penetrated MI6 as well as the Foreign Office."

C held up his hand toward Philby and indicated an inch with his fingers. "Such a pity about Volkov," he said with frustration." We were *that* close..."

2

Not long afterwards Philby accepted Angleton's invitation to go fly-fishing in Virginia. As the two stood side by side in the midst of a cold trout stream on a spring afternoon, it seemed to Philby a pleasant diversion from all the recent intrigue. Or so he thought until Angleton shot him an inquisitive look.

"Do you think it's worth it?" asked Angleton, as he cast his line.

"What's that?" replied Philby warily.

"All the lost souls."

Philby cast his line in turn. "Albania, you mean?"

Angleton sighed. "I mean the whole shebang. Dulles says this 'game' we're playing is the real war. But do you really think any of this is making the least bit of difference?"

"I should hope so. But isn't this about the larger struggle?"

Angleton jerked back his line. "Damn! Nearly had 'em. And what struggle is that?"

"The struggle for a better world," replied Philby, carefully. "Democracy and all that."

"Yeah. But I guess it depends on how you define *all* that."

"I'm afraid you've lost me there, Jim."

"Have I? Whoa, grab the net!" A large rainbow trout leaped from the churning water a few yards in front of them. It fought ferociously for a few minutes until Angleton gradually pulled it in. Philby splashed through the water towards it and netted the fish. "Nice one!"

On the drive home on a rural highway, the men were silent for a while until Angleton turned to Philby and started to quote.

"Knowing others is wisdom; knowing yourself is enlightenment."

"Shakespeare?" guessed Philby.

"Lao Tzu." Angleton looked inquisitively at Philby. "Do you ever feel like you've lost your soul? When we spend our life deceiving others, how do we keep from deceiving ourselves? The drug of deceit can be fatal."

A moment of silence passed as both men looked out thoughtfully at the passing countryside. Philby turned and looked at Angleton.

"So how did you ever get into this business?" asked Angleton.

"Playing the 'Great Game,' you mean? College. There were a number of active political societies when I was up at Cambridge, and I wanted to find some way to make a difference."

"Cambridge! But weren't there lots of communist cells there in the thirties? The 'Apostles' for one?"

Philby flashed Angleton a suspicious glance. "I suppose. Communism at the time seemed the only real bulwark against the rise of Fascism."

"Heaven forbid *you* ever associated with those Commie scum?"

Philby laughed. "Heaven forbid indeed!"

"I know."

Philby shot a surprised glance at Angleton, who returned a cunning grin. "I checked," he said.

The next morning Philby sat in the FBI Headquarters conferring with Hoover.

"I heard about Albania," growled Hoover, as he puffed a fat cigar and exhaled a cloud of smoke so thick Philby feared he might suffocate.

Philby coughed. "That was a real tragedy."

"It was more than that! It means our mole is privy to a lot more than the workings of the embassy kitchen. You can't find out about sensitive CIA operations just by digging through their dumpster. Trust me, I've tried." Hoover stood up and paced around Philby as he continued. "Now, what progress have you made with that list of suspects I gave you?"

"I've got a few leads. But I'm still building a case. I need a little more time to investigate."

Hoover stooped down and glared at Philby, blowing another smoke cloud directly into his face. "And that's the one thing we don't have. Ask me for money, power, facilities, you name it and it's yours courtesy of the US Government. But time has run out!"

Philby struggled not to cough in Hoover's face. "I understand."

"I hope you do. 'Cause while we sit here shittin' around, some goddamn compatriot of yours is compromising United States security!" Philby maintained a stoic silence in the face of Hoover's tirade.

"And," persisted Hoover, "I expect you to blow both his identity and his ass to kingdom come before we expel the whole pack of you. Understood?"

"Understood." Philby got up to leave.

"And Philby?"

"Yes?"

"Don't forget they can be anywhere."

"Who's that, sir?"

"The Ruskies. Don't let 'em fool you. They can be anybody, anywhere."

3

Even as Hoover spoke, Natasha stood in a Paris flat applying crimson red lipstick in front of a bathroom mirror. She was wrapped in a towel, and in the mirror she could see Sergei Gurushina approaching naked from behind her. She smiled as he wrapped his arms around her and kissed her neck while removing the towel and fondling her breasts. She turned around and seductively moved toward the bed.

At sunset, when Natasha stood at the doorway preparing to leave, Gurushina helped her into her jacket. She picked up her purse and umbrella and opened the door. But just before leaving, she reached into her purse and took out a red, heart-shaped box, handing it to him with a sweet smile. He started to open it, but she gently stopped him with a touch of her hand. Then she spoke, now with a sensual French accent.

"For you, mon chéri. It is a surprise!"

Gurushina smiled silently as Natasha kissed him good-bye and stepped out into the busy Place de la Bastille. He watched a moment, quite pleased with himself. Then he sat down on a couch by the living room window and opened the box. He sniffed the contents and smiled contentedly, but then squinted with alarm at the message written on the scarlet red paper lining the chocolates. It read "From Russia With Love."

When Gurushina had carefully lifted the lining, he sighed with relief only to find a layer of colorful chocolates. He smiled as he lifted a heart-shaped candy out of the box. Suddenly, a ticking sound started from within the box and he saw thin copper wires protruding from the spot where the piece of chocolate had been. In a panic Gurushina dumped out the rest of the chocolate to find a small time bomb taped inside. The needle had just ticked to three seconds from zero.

Outside, Natasha continued her brisk, carefree strut across Place de la Bastille, her face expressionless apart from the wry smile frozen on her lips. She did not look back or even flinch when a sudden blast rocked the street behind her, where a plume of black smoke began to pour thickly from the shattered windows of Gurushina's flat.

4

In London, Guy Burgess was throwing himself a grand farewell party. In attendance was an odd assortment of London society representing his wide (and rather bizarre) circle of friends, from posh Oxbridge-trained diplomatic types to "rough trade" from the street. And among the guests was Anthony Blunt.

Burgess sat on a couch, one hand holding a drink and the other affectionately around the neck of his housemate and lover Jack Hewit. Hewit held an opium pipe, and between long puffs chatted loquaciously in his thick cockney accent.

"You'd better be bloody careful over in America, mate."

"Of what, pray tell?" replied Burgess. "The sordid temptations of the bourgeoisie?"

"You know what I mean, Guy. Your mouth, for one. I hear all it takes is a word about communism, or homosexuality, and they'll throw you in the fryer. Just like that!"

"What you're trying to say, dear boy," answered Burgess, "is this: 'For God's sake, Guy, whatever you do don't make a pass at Joseph McCarthy!'"

Burgess saw Blunt approaching. "Ah Anthony, you're just in time to defend me from Jack's scandalous insinuations about me. He's accusing me of being both a Communist *and* a homosexual!"

"Heaven forbid!" commented Blunt.

"And he nevertheless seems to hold the preposterous view that such inclinations don't represent the American majority."

"Then he is nothing if not profoundly mistaken!" laughed Blunt. "But it's all one in the States. Try not to preach against racism though, or you'll be arrested for heresy."

Hewit took another deep puff from his pipe and shook his head in disbelief. "Blimey!"

Blunt touched Burgess' shoulder. "Guy, a brief word outside, if I may?"

Burgess nodded to Hewit and followed Blunt outside to the back porch, where he lit a cigarette. Blunt looked around carefully before reaching inside his coat. Burgess watched as Blunt pulled something from an inner pocket and concealed it in his hand.

"I have something for you." Blunt pulled Burgess into an embrace and slipped the object into his friend's hand. Then he looked at Burgess intimately. "You know what to do." Burgess nodded with a smile.

A week later Burgess was settling into his new post in Washington—and, despite Aileen Philby's fervent displeasure—his lodgings in the guest room of the Philbys' home near the British Embassy. Where, soon afterwards, the ambassador held a reception in the Embassy garden.

At the reception Philby stood speaking with both Maclean and Burgess, while Aileen and Melinda stood just apart from their husbands in front of a string quartet performing Vivaldi's "Autumn." Angleton, from across the garden, observed with keen interest as Maclean's expression suddenly became serious.

The ambassador began to clink on his glass and there was an immediate hush from the crowd as all turned toward him.

"Ladies and Gentlemen, welcome," he began. "I shall keep this quite brief, and I trust people come to such occasions rather more for diplomatic hospitality than for diplomatic speeches." A polite chuckle trickled around the garden. "But I should like to take a moment to toast the two individuals in whose honor we're gathered here this afternoon. Indeed, this occasion is at the same time both a farewell and a welcome." The ambassador looked toward Burgess as he continued, unable to conceal a look of disapproval. "As the Bard himself might put it, 'the funeral baked meats do coldly furnish forth the marriage tables.'"

This provoked muted laughter from the crowd, and a mischievous smirk from Burgess as the ambassador concluded his speech.

"And so without further ado, and with the added benefit of killing two toasts with one drink, I salute both Donald Maclean and Guy Burgess. The former for his esteemed service as His Majesty's First Secretary in Washington, and with best wishes for his new posting to Cairo. And the latter in warm welcome as Donald's replacement from the Foreign Office." The ambassador raised his glass.

"Long live the King!"

"Long live the King!" all toasted in unison.

Within another week Donald and Melinda Maclean had arrived in Cairo, where the two sat in their new garden sipping wine beneath fragrant pink mimosa blossoms flowering over the veranda. Maclean held their one-year old son in his lap, whom he smiled at wistfully. He might even have seemed fully content were it not for his foot twitching nervously up and down, coupled with his morose expression. Melinda observed him with a deepening frown.

Maclean carefully stood up with the baby and sat him gently in Melinda's lap. She flashed a sarcastic smile. "More work again tonight?"

"Just a bit… but I'll be done with it soon."

"You said things would be different here, Donald."

"They will, darling. I just need a little more time."

"Time? When will you ever have time for me?" She looked quickly at the baby. "For *us?*"

A look of pain filled Maclean's face. There was nothing he could say, and he knew he had only one last chance to make things right.

"I just have to take care of some business first. Trust me, Mel."

"Business! Do you give a damn about us at all, Donald?" The baby started to cry, and Melinda attempted to console him while continuing to glare at her husband.

"I do indeed," Maclean said quietly. "More than I can possibly explain." He smiled awkwardly and turned away.

A little later he sat on a bench perched along the Nile riverbank. And sitting next to Maclean was an ominous figure wearing a large fedora pulled down low over his face, in a heavy trench coat despite the warm season. It was his Soviet Control, and Maclean spoke to him quickly and anxiously, all the while staring ahead as if watching the barges drifting languidly past along the river.

"I want out," stated Maclean, a hint of desperation in his voice.

"Out?"

"I've had enough of this double life. The strain is intolerable. I have a wife, a child…"

"Your commitment to us was for life," replied the Control, speaking slowly and carefully, his thick Russian accent sounding particularly ominous to Maclean on this occasion.

"I was just a boy, young and idealistic. I didn't know what I know now."

"And what *do* you now know?"

Maclean looked nervously over his shoulder, his eyes darting frantically in every direction apart from that of the man next to him. "I think they're on to me."

"We are aware of this. Do not worry, my friend, everything will be taken care of."

"But I don't *want* anything else 'taken care of' — I just want out!"

"That," replied the Control, calmly and decisively, "is the one thing you cannot have. You have chosen your path, and it leads in only one direction." Maclean finally turned toward the man and stared at him imploringly, but the Control abruptly stood up.

"There is no out," he muttered under his breath, and with that he turned his back to Maclean and walked swiftly away along the river.

Maclean dropped his head into his hands and began to cry softly, anxiously pulling his wedding band up and down along his finger.

"Oh God, what have I done?" he sighed.

5

On the afternoon of June 25TH, 1950, the Philby family—now including Burgess, lolling on the floor with a bottle of wine in one hand and a cigarette in the other—gathered around the television as a news flash announced the start of hostilities in Korea:

"The North Korean Communist army struck in the pre-dawn hours this morning. Equipped with Soviet weaponry and tanks, they crossed the thirty-eighth parallel behind a fire storm of artillery barrage. President Truman has secured UN approval to order U.S. naval and air forces to stem the North Korean advance. General Douglas MacArthur has moved troops . . ."

Philby, sitting in his armchair thoughtfully puffing his pipe, scowled. "Two years of covert operations there, and CIA didn't see it coming."

Burgess barked a sarcastic laugh. "Bloody hell! Are the wankers trying to start World War III?"

Aileen gave Philby a sharp look, nodding towards the children listening attentively from the couch.

"Guy," murmured Philby.

But Burgess persisted. "Haven't the Yanks got better things to do with their resources than bomb helpless peasants?"

"Guy!" insisted Philby, a little louder.

"Oh, right!" relented Burgess. "Sorry old man, the children and all that. But what do you think about all this?"

Philby glanced carefully toward Aileen. "It's not for us to decide that, is it? Our hands are tied by the Foreign Office."

Burgess became angry. "In other words, we're at His Majesty's leisure, you might say. What a load of bollocks!" Hearing Aileen sigh audibly, Burgess added: "Oh, sorry!" Then he got up and stormed out. But just as Aileen appeared to relax, he popped his head back into the living room. "What time's the party?"

"Eightish," answered Philby.

"Right, cheers. Ta!"

As they heard Burgess start to descend the stairs to his basement room, Aileen called after him: "But I thought you said you weren't coming!" There came no reply, and she turned a concerned gaze to her husband. "I thought you said he wasn't coming?"

"Don't worry darling, he'll be fine. Now I've got to leg it or I shall be late for my first meeting!" Philby saw the look of exasperation in his wife's face as he gave her a quick kiss on the cheek.

"Kim?" she called, but the only response was the front door slamming shut as he left.

A few minutes later Philby sat once again with Angleton at Harvey's Restaurant. The waiter approached the table and looked first at Angleton.

"The usual sir?"

"The usual. Two."

The waiter nodded and prepared to leave, but Philby stopped him. "Just the tail for me, please!"

"Very good, sir," nodded the waiter, before hastening briskly away.

Philby smiled at Angleton. "Our weekly gastronomic adventures have taken a toll. My scale informs me I now weigh thirteen stone!"

Angleton chuckled. "Then you need to exercise more than your mind, my friend."

"Ah yes, gardening. How's yours coming along? Still struggling with *moles?*"

"Funny you should ask," said Angleton, barely masking a cunning smile, "as I think I may be on the verge of eradicating them completely."

"Is that so?"

"Yep. In fact, I think I've narrowed them down to an exact number: *Five.*"

Philby dropped his fork in a rare loss of composure, but quickly recovered. "A good natural number, I suppose!" he replied good-naturedly.

Angleton abruptly dropped his metaphorical game and got to the point. "You see Kim, I believe Hoover's up to something he hasn't informed CIA about."

"Indeed."

A pause followed, as Philby confronted the intensity of

Angleton's gaze. And then the coup de grâce.

"Homer," said Angleton.

"Sorry?"

"And I don't mean Troy." Angleton leaned in closer over the table. "I'm convinced there's a mole in the British Secret Service. Someone high up in MI6. And I'm going to catch him if it's the last thing I do."

Soon after lunch the two men sat in the office of CIA Deputy Director Dulles, who puffed his cigar thoughtfully while explaining his vision of the New Order.

"…which I'm calling 'weapons of mass destruction' for lack of a better phrase. Gentlemen, such a weapon in the hands of Communists is the greatest threat the world has ever faced."

Philby shook his head. "But they already have the bomb. Isn't it rather late to try to stop them?"

"They have the bomb," Dulles concurred, "but one or two bombs hardly concerns us. As long as they know, or think at least, that we have an equal number of such weapons to use in a counterattack, then we're safe from attack ourselves. In theory, at least."

Angleton nodded. "Keeping the idea of all-out war not only 'cold' but in a perpetual deep freeze."

Dulles took a moment to process Angleton's analogy. "Yes," he continued, "assuming the Russians aren't barbaric enough to strike first without provocation from us."

"And likewise," responded Philby, "precluding a first strike by the United States."

Dulles looked at Philby incredulously for a moment and then cleared his throat. "Intelligence suggests the Russians are having difficulty finding uranium. They've got slave laborers in Czechoslovakia digging out rock with their bare hands. But apparently all they've found there is a few pounds of the pure stuff."

"What would it take to support a full-scale atomic program?" asked Philby.

"At least a hundred tons of high-grade uranium. We're planning a clandestine operation to investigate suspected processing plants. Both to confirm they *are* processing uranium, and to ascertain which process they're using if so."

"Paratroopers?" asked Angleton.

"Precisely. They'll be dropped by night at geographical coordinates inside unguarded stretches of the Soviet border. Once again I'm placing you gentlemen in joint command of planning the operation." Dulles looked down for a moment before proceeding. "We're taking every precaution to protect this from leaks. There's been suspicion that the Albania mission got blown on this end."

Angleton and Philby traded quick glances.

"When do we launch?" asked Philby.

"Late May."

With a nod Dulles indicated the meeting was adjourned, and the men got up to leave. "Angleton, could I have a quick word?"

Angleton and Philby exchanged nods as Philby exited the office and closed the door. Angleton sat down again and looked at Dulles questioningly.

"I want you to keep an eye on Philby," said Dulles, shaking his head doubtfully. "There's something not quite right about him."

"Yes, sir."

Outside in the hallway, Philby overheard this conversation through the door before quietly slipping away down the hallway.

***

Philby's final stop that afternoon was the one he dreaded most. The moment he stepped into Hoover's office and sat down, a folder marked "TOP SECRET" was thrust in his face.

"Here's the updated list," announced Hoover. "We've narrowed the suspects down to nine from almost nine-hundred embassy employees. Each of the remaining suspects is a top British official."

Philby quickly skimmed down the list with his forefinger until stopping at the name *Maclean, Donald*. Then he looked back up at Hoover. "I'll keep each of them under close surveillance, sir. I shall report back to you in due course."

Hoover nodded skeptically and Philby got up to leave, but Hoover called after him: "Why do you think it is that the Soviets seem as worried about you Brits as about us?"

Philby turned around and smiled. "SIS wasn't ten years old when it got a shot at Lenin in 1918. Had the bugger died, there would have been no Soviet Union. Good afternoon, sir." Philby turned to leave, but Hoover wasn't finished.

"Oh, and Philby?"

Philby reluctantly turned back around. "Sir?"

"Keep an eye out for someone who's unstable, living on his nerves. A non-conformist. That'll be our man."

"Suspicion always haunts the guilty mind," quoted Philby, hastening out of the office lest Hoover think of anything more to add.

As if on cue, on the other side of the world Maclean stood holding court in the midst of the Nile on a yacht, the site of a posh diplomatic party cruise. And where a drunken Maclean had all but lost complete self-control.

"The hypocrisy of it all!" he exhorted. "London says we're here to 'further the well-being of the peoples of the Middle East.' What a load of shite! The real motive is the expansion of British oil companies in the region."

Melinda gently took Maclean's arm and tried to restrain him. "Donald."

Maclean angrily shook her off and continued his rant. "I mean, when you think about it we're no better than the bloody Yanks. Britain wouldn't give a donkey's arse about the Middle East if it weren't for the oil…"

"Donald!" objected Melinda.

"Christ woman, bugger off, will you? Here…" He drained his drink and held the glass out to her. "Why don't you get me another G&T while you're at it?"

"And why don't you go to hell!" Melinda retorted. She turned her back to him and started to walk away. But Maclean grabbed his wife and roughly pulled her backwards while the other passengers watched this spectacle in horror. "Leave your fucking attitude at home," he shouted. "I'll teach you to play the tart with me in public!"

Melinda screamed as Maclean started to throttle her, and an Egyptian guard ran out of the cabin with a rifle. Maclean suddenly turned and grabbed the rifle, pushing the guard over the railing and into the water. Then he began swinging the rifle in arcs over his head at imaginary attackers until another guard emerged and tackled Maclean from behind, attempting to wrestle the rifle away from him. Maclean fell backwards on top of the guard, firing the rifle harmlessly toward the sky before finally dropping the gun and passing out in a drunken stupor.

6

In the Philbys' living room, a fire blazed as Aileen bustled around the room filling wine glasses. She was no stranger to hosting diplomatic soirées for her husband's colleagues, but the presence this time of senior American officials seemed to raise the stakes with regard to proper etiquette in a strange land. Now she was understandably high-strung as she stood speaking with the British Ambassador, keeping watch with one eye as Philby in turn proved the ever-gracious host while making rounds with the martini pitcher. He noticed Angleton alone in a corner scanning the living room bookshelves, where he seemed especially interested in several large red volumes labeled *The Collected Works of Karl Marx.*

When Philby saw his wife chatting with the ambassador, he joined them. "Another martini, Mr. Ambassador?"

"Don't mind if I do!"

As he filled the ambassador's glass, Philby saw Aileen look suddenly across the room with alarm. "Oh lord!" she gasped. The men followed her gaze to see that Burgess had just entered. He was disheveled and obviously quite drunk.

The ambassador frowned. "Whoever had the lunatic idea of sending that man to Washington is beyond my guess. His debauchery is well-known in Whitehall."

"Then perhaps they thought he'd fit right in here," said Philby.

"Oh well, I suppose he could be worse." The ambassador shook his head with resigned disapproval. But Aileen gestured in exasperation. "What could be worse? Goats?"

As they watched, Burgess poured himself a drink from a bottle of bourbon at the bar and knocked it back. The ambassador turned again to Philby. "It was certainly quite noble of you to put him up."

"He's an old friend, and I thought I should keep an eye on him, too. He's all right."

"He's here most days," interjected Aileen. "Getting pissed and playing with our little boy's toy trains in the basement."

At that moment a tipsy young woman came up to Burgess and tapped him on the shoulder. He looked up and smiled. "Hullo, my good lady, and what may I do for you? Within reason, of course." Burgess winked at her.

"Mr. Burgess, I've heard you're a brilliant caricaturist, and I was wondering if you might draw me?"

"Within *reason* I said! The only thing I'll draw for you is a drink. Now, what will you have?" With that Burgess turned back to the bar and poured himself another drink. When he turned back around he appeared visibly annoyed that the lady still stood there, regarding him expectantly.

"Please Mr. Burgess. It's for my husband."

"And might I ask who is so lucky to possess such a re-sistible lady?"

"Bill Harvey," she stammered. "He works with CIA."

"Ah! The gentleman who got sacked by Hoover for drunk-enness on duty? In that case I shall be most delighted to draw you!" Burgess smiled facetiously as he took out a pad and pen from his breast pocket. "Now, my dear, please just give me your sweetest and most lascivious pose."

The lady smiled as Burgess sat her in a chair. He ap-peared to be a study in concentration, intent on producing a fine work of art. First he framed her face with a theatrical air as she preened with anticipation. After a few minutes of drawing, he stepped back and looked from his pad to the lady in comparison. "Perfect!" he gleefully announced. Then he held up the result for her to see. "Your husband will be charmed, I'm sure."

The moment she saw it she screamed with shock. The drawing depicted her in the nude, her legs spread wide.

"Shockingly good, isn't it?" giggled Burgess.

Philby and Aileen rushed toward them, followed closely by Bill Harvey—who shouted to his wife as he strode across the room: "Libby?!"

Libby Harvey stood staring at the picture in disbelief. "I've never been so insulted in my life!" When her husband saw the picture he glared at Burgess, still gloating in amusement with pen and pad in hand.

"Why you!" shouted Harvey. He punched Burgess in the face, almost knocking him into the fireplace. Philby stood between them, trying to shield Burgess from Harvey's further wrath. "It was just a bad joke," he explained. "He didn't mean any harm."

"Sure fella, just a bad joke." Harvey took a deep breath and regained self-control before turning back to his wife. "Come on honey, let's get outta here!"

As they left, Aileen looked at the picture Burgess had drawn; then she looked at Burgess and finally released with a loud shriek all the repressed anger that had built up since his arrival. She stared at Philby in contempt. "I've had enough, Kim! You're more loyal to him than you've ever been to me!"

She stormed out of the house and slammed the door behind her, as shocked guests stood still in embarrassed silence. Meanwhile the unrepentant Burgess simply helped himself to another drink.

Angleton observed Philby quickly disappear into the kitchen after his wife's outburst. He followed a few minutes later, and when he entered the kitchen stopped short in dismay. There was Kim Philby, pride of the British Secret Service and the man never known to lose his self-control, sitting with his head cradled in his hands—and weeping.

"How could you, how could you, how could you?" Philby lamented. "Everything's going horribly wrong..." When Philby at last looked up, he saw Angleton standing there, thoughtfully watching him.

Later that evening, after all the guests had hastily departed and Philby had gathered his wits, he sat with Burgess in the dying firelight drinking in silence. They sat that way a long while until they saw the glare of headlights and heard a car pull into the driveway. The door opened and Aileen stumbled in. She was covered in blood.

Philby jumped up. "Aileen! What happened, dear?"

"An accident..." she mumbled. "It's nothing, don't worry about me."

"But..."

Aileen ran past her husband and into the bathroom, where she closed and locked the door behind her and began to sob. Philby went outside and looked at the car but could see no damage apart from blood in the front seat. He returned inside, sat back down in front of the fireplace, and took a deep drink.

Burgess stared at him. "My God, Kim, what happened? Was she in a motorcar accident? Is she all right?"

Philby shook his head as he stared towards the fire, now just a flickering glow of dying embers. The sound of Aileen sobbing in the bathroom had also faded to a soft whimper.

"It wasn't an accident," he said softly. "Or rather, not an unintentional one. Her mother once told me that when Aileen was a child, whenever she felt neglected she'd injure herself." Philby dropped his head in anguish. "How could I have been so blind?" He hit the arm of his chair and looked up at Burgess. "How can we have been so blind?"

7

When Melinda Maclean walked into a Cairo bar in search of her husband, she found him raving drunk and in a fight. She watched in dismay as a bouncer grabbed Maclean from behind in a futile attempt to stop the fighting.

"Get your hands off me, you bugger!" Maclean shouted. "I'm a bloody Soviet agent, and the Russians'll have your balls!" He wrested himself free from the bouncer and ran to the bar, where he stood uncontrollably smashing glasses against the wall until someone finally knocked him over the head with a bottle. He immediately fell unconscious to the floor.

In a dream Maclean found himself standing with Melinda on the banks of the Seine in Paris. He could hear the sound of distant gunfire as smoke swirled up from around the Parisian suburbs.

There's only one way we can leave together, he heard himself saying, taking her hand. Marry me, Melinda!
Marry you? But we hardly know each other!
It doesn't matter. I love you, I'll love you forever.
I don't know, Donald, I have to think...
There's no time to think, we have to leave now before the Nazis enter Paris!
Where will we go?
There's a British destroyer docked at Saint-Tropez. We can travel together as long as we can prove we're man and wife. It's

now or never, darling. If we don't get married now, we might never see each other again!

Donald…

"Donald!"

Maclean opened his eyes, and Melinda stood over him, holding his hand. After a few moments he knew he was in a hospital room, and why. He smiled at his wife shyly.

"I've been a real cock-up, haven't I?"

"I spoke to the ambassador. To avoid a 'diplomatic incident,' you're being recalled to London at once."

"London? But why?"

"You'll get help there…"

"Help?"

Maclean attempted to sit up in bed, but Melinda gently pushed his head back onto the pillow. "You can't say you don't need it! But they think it's just overwork."

Maclean sat up again. "But my work!"

His wife attempted a smile. "The good news is that, when they think you're fit for work again, you'll be back in the Foreign Office."

"Doing what?"

"The ambassador says with your Washington experience, you'll be head of the American Department." She turned to go, but Maclean reached out and touched her sleeve.

"Mel?"

"What?"

"I love you…"

Melinda gave him another pained smile as he looked at her intently. "Do you even know me anymore?" she asked.

"I don't even know myself. But Mel, there's something I need to tell you."

Even as Maclean felt an inkling of hope well up in his breast, an altogether different fate was being woven for him by events in Washington. There, a cryptographer sat in the basement of the FBI headquarters busily comparing documents from the 'Venona' decrypts. One document contained the phrases *New York family* and *Homer's American wife*. He compared this with another document describing "Donald D. Maclean" along with his mug shot. The cryptographer taped all these together to complete the puzzle. Then he picked up the phone.

PART IV

I

One evening in early May 1951, Philby and Burgess sat watching Senator Joseph McCarthy speaking on television, almost shouting as his words poured forth his darkest suspicions:

"…a great conspiracy, a conspiracy so immense as to dwarf any previous such venture in the history of man. A conspiracy of infamy so black that, when it is finally exposed, its principals shall be forever deserving of the maledictions of all honest men…"

Burgess sat cross-legged on the floor with his usual cigarette and drink. "What a wanker!" he commented. "They're using communism as an excuse to keep people in a grip of fear."

"Who constitutes the highest circles of this conspiracy? About that we cannot be sure. The President? He is their captive."

"Can't the people see it's only about control?" continued Burgess. "They swallow government propaganda like blind sheep. Can't they see this whole 'War on Communism' thing keeps idiots like that in power?"

Philby appeared thoughtful, and murmured to himself: "The only thing we have to fear is fear itself. How easily people forget that in a climate of reaction."

"Yes indeed. It's frightening how a supposedly sophisticated electorate is so easy to fool."

"...only dimly aware of what is going on. I don't believe that Mr. Truman is a conscious party to the great conspiracy, although it is being conducted in his name. I believe that if Mr. Truman had the ability to associate good Americans around him, he would have behaved as a good American in this most dire of all our crises..."

Burgess stood up in anger. "This country's being driven by the military machine. What America needs is a stiff dose of socialism!"

The next day when Philby walked into the FBI Director's office, Hoover promptly held up a tape recorder and pushed the play button. From the speaker came Burgess' inimitable voice:

"What America needs is a stiff dose of socialism."

Hoover stopped the tape and sat at his desk. "And what do you have to say about that, Mr. Philby?"

Philby stared at the tape player a moment incredulously. "You're still bugging my house! But you said..."

"I know what I said. But that was before I started getting unsavory reports concerning your housemate."

"What sort of reports?"

Hoover scowled. "That he's a known homosexual, for one. His indiscretions around Washington are no secret. And speaking of secrets, when he's drunk, he'd tell any transvestite in town every secret he knows. Including the real names of our agents."

"I want to know how you can legally bug my house!" Philby demanded. "Isn't unwarranted surveillance against your precious Constitution?"

"We're at war, son. In a time of crisis the Constitution's meaningless. I wouldn't hesitate to spy on anyone I damn well please."

Philby stuck his tongue squarely in his cheek. "God help America if it ever gets a President without respect for the Constitution."

Hoover smirked. "What I want to know is why you're harboring a drunk homosexual socialist in your home?"

"I have a duty to my friends, sir."

"And you have a duty to me as MI6 liaison officer to the FBI!"

"Yes, sir."

"It's also your duty to inform me the moment Mr. Burgess, friend or no friend, decides it's his duty to criticize our government."

Philby resisted his strong urge to challenge Hoover, and instead nodded in silence as Hoover continued.

"In the meantime 'Homer' is still on the prowl and it's high time we cornered the asshole. You're supposed to be the expert on Soviet counter-intelligence, so where's our man?" Hoover handed Philby a document. "I don't know what you've been doing with your time, Philby, but on this end we've narrowed the list down to five."

Philby glanced over the list, and Maclean was still on it.

"And out of these, we're pretty sure we've got our man in the bag."

"What a coincidence," smiled Philby, "as I was about to report the same conclusion from my end."

Hoover's office wasn't the only place that day in which the person of interest was Maclean. He was also the topic on a London park bench, where Anthony Blunt sat in Regent's Park conferring with his Soviet Control, Yuri Modin. A passerby would have assumed the two men complete strangers: Modin appeared to be ensconced in reading *The Times*, while Blunt had his head buried in a first edition of *1984*. The two men nonetheless managed to swap a brief but weighty exchange.

"Our Scottish lamb's in need of a shepherd," muttered Blunt. "He's much too fragile on his own."

Modin glanced furtively aside to Blunt. "Do you have someone in mind?"

Blunt nodded in affirmation. Then he closed his book and walked briskly away.

Oblivious to all the unwanted attention he was receiving, Maclean worked busily late into each night at the British Foreign Office in London—busy with his KGB wallet-camera, photographing documents on Anglo-American atomic weapons research and war plans. Yet his hands trembled so badly that he could hardly function. A growing sense of dread in his gut warned him that something was about to happen. But what it was he could hardly guess.

2

Burgess lolled carelessly one afternoon on the Philby basement floor near an impressive model train set. The tracks occupied a large portion of the room, and young John Philby watched excitedly as Burgess carefully placed a car he had just repaired on the track and attached it to the train's engine car.

"Will it go now?" asked John.

"Yes indeed, my boy, just press this button."

John pressed the button and he and Burgess were equally thrilled as the train took off around the tracks. Burgess took a celebratory swig from a bottle of Jack Daniels as Aileen appeared at the bottom of the stairs and frowned. She held out a letter to Burgess.

"How many times have I asked you not to drink in front of John?" she complained.

"Oh, terribly sorry, we were just…"

"I can see what you're doing. Don't they ever miss you at the Embassy?"

"I'm on diplomatic leave to assist Mr. Philby here in repairing the Santa Fe line. Very important work too, isn't it John?"

John grinned. "Yes Mummy, me and Mr. Burgess…"

"Mr. Burgess and *I*," corrected Aileen.

"Mr. Burgess and I fixed the train!"

Aileen forced a smile for her son. "Very impressive dear. There was a letter for you in the box, Guy." She handed Burgess the letter. "At least I assume it's for you. It's unstamped and just has your initials on it. No return address."

"Cheers," said Burgess, looking curiously at the envelope. Then he winced upon seeing the letters 'GB' handwritten on the envelope in red ink.

That night Burgess stealthily entered a dark Washington alley, where from out of the shadows stepped Anatoli Golitsin in a long grey overcoat. Burgess guessed this was his Soviet Washington Control by the stubbly beard he wore beneath his sharp Slavic nose, and he reached in his pocket and took out a puzzle piece, which connected with Golitsin's to complete yet another of the Kremlin's five stars.

"You must accompany Homer," said Golitsin.

"But how? I don't have any excuse to leave Washington."

"Then you must get yourself reassigned."

"Get myself reassigned," Burgess murmured quietly to himself. Then he smiled knowingly. The two men nodded, and without speaking they each turned simultaneously and walked away in opposite directions.

In the shadows across the street, however, stood Angleton, lurking unseen as he watched the two men intently.

The next day Burgess switched on the ignition of his Lincoln Continental convertible and revved up the motor. Aileen looked through the front window just in time to see him tear out of the driveway with the top down.

Burgess took an exit ramp and cruised down the freeway. He wore designer shades and smoked a cigarette, weaving through traffic with his radio blaring out the latest rock n' roll hits. A policeman parked along the shoulder looked up in alarm as Burgess flew past. He hit his siren and lights and tore after the speeding Lincoln.

Minutes later the officer stood looking with amazement at Burgess's passport.

"Diplomat, eh?"

"Yessiree!" squealed Burgess like a delighted child.

"Urgent business or something? I clocked you going nearly ninety!"

"Oh wow! I'd no idea this baby could cruise so *fast!*" commented Burgess, putting on his most outrageous American accent. "Cool!"

The officer frowned as he wrote on a ticket and handed it to Burgess. "Here's a warning, sir. Please try to slow down."

"Sure thing, sir!"

But just as the officer turned away, Burgess put pedal to metal and screeched back onto the freeway.

"Hey!" the officer shouted, running back to his car and again taking off after Burgess with lights and siren whining down the freeway.

A day later Burgess sat in the British Ambassador's office receiving an official reprimand. The ambassador frowned at him from across his wide desk.

"This is disgraceful. Three speeding tickets in one day! What the devil were you thinking, Burgess?"

"They were only warnings, sir. I do have diplomatic immunity."

The ambassador's frown deepened to a scowl. "That's beside the point. The Governor of Virginia himself sent a protest about you to the State Department. He's furious about this flagrant abuse of diplomatic privilege."

"Oh dear..."

"But this is only the tip of the iceberg as far as we're concerned. You've single-handedly managed to insult about everyone in Washington, apart from the President himself—which I'm sure you would do if given the opportunity."

Burgess struggled to suppress a smile as the ambassador glared at him.

"The truth is, Burgess, you've worn out your welcome here.

Both in Washington and at this Embassy. Ever since you got here, you've been on an odyssey of indiscretions. And I'd be exaggerating if I said it was with regret that you're being recalled to London. Well, what have you got to say for yourself?"

Burgess pouted. "Obviously I'm devastated, sir."

"Obviously," the ambassador sighed.

Two days later Aileen Philby stood at the window watching expressionlessly as her husband helped Burgess load up the car. Philby slammed the car trunk shut and then turned to Burgess and grinned.

"Ready?" he asked.

Burgess nodded and turned to open the car door. As he did so he caught a glimpse of Aileen in the window, who quickly drew the curtains and vanished. But when the car started, she glanced back out and watched as Philby pulled out of the driveway and disappeared around the corner.

When Philby arrived at the FBI headquarters that afternoon, Hoover angrily rubber stamped an "FBI Wanted" document and handed it to him. The mug shot of the suspect was that of Donald Maclean. Philby nodded.

Hoover picked up the phone. "Get me London. MI5 HQ," he demanded, chomping a cigar impatiently.

3

"There's serious trouble."

Anthony Blunt looked anxiously at Yuri Modin. The two men stood on the back of a tour boat gliding along the Thames, and were just passing by the Tower of London.

"Homer is about to be arrested and interrogated by MI5," Blunt explained. "But he's in such a state I'm convinced he'll break down under questioning."

"Then he must defect to Moscow immediately."

Blunt shook his head. "Burgess is back and says Maclean can't bring himself to leave his family."

Modin frowned coldly. "There is no option. He must defect or we are all in jeopardy. Burgess will escort him."

Blunt shot his comrade a questioning look.

Modin stared out across the river toward London Bridge. "Moscow now sees him too as a liability to our work."

Philby stood the next morning in front of the ambassador's desk, who promptly slapped down a newspaper.

"The bird has flown."

"What bird?" asked Philby.

The ambassador handed him the newspaper. It was *The Washington Post* of June 8, 1951. The headline read: "TWO BRITISH DIPLOMATS 'DISSAPEAR' IN EUROPE; FLIGHT TO RUSSIA FEARED. Both Served Here. Acheson Regards Desertions By Britons As Serious If True."

Philby gave a look of dawning horror. "Not Maclean?"

"Yes. But unfortunately that's not the half of it. Guy Burgess is with him." He indicated the newspaper article.

"The media seem to know more about it than we do!"

"Burgess? But why?"

The ambassador regarded Philby curiously. "Apparently, that is a question MI5's hoping you can help answer." He handed Philby a letter. "You're expected in London immediately."

Just down the street, Hoover furiously waved the same newspaper at an assistant.

"That son-of-a-bitch Maclean knew everything! He was the Brits' atomic energy man in Washington. He had access to highly classified material at the Atomic Energy Commission, and he even had an all-access pass to AEC headquarters. Even *I* had to have an appointment and an escort to enter there! What the hell is this? How'd they ever let him slip?"

Hoover paced frantically around his office while his young assistant watched with helpless silence. Hoover's expression transformed to a look of deep suspicion.

"And where the fuck is Philby? How could a spy be living undetected in the house of a trained counter-intelligence officer?" Hoover looked imploringly at the assistant.

"He's been recalled to London, sir."

Hoover appeared thunderstruck. "London?"

At CIA headquarters, an incredulous Dulles was just posing the same question to Angleton.

"London?"

Dulles stood behind his desk holding the identical headline and glaring at Angleton.

"I'll be meeting with him for a drink before he leaves, sir."

Dulles nodded. "Then find out all you can." He stared with exasperation again at the headline. "Goddammit, Angleton! It would seem their head of Russian counter-intelligence *is* Russian Intelligence. The 'Russian Problem' just got a lot more difficult…"

Shortly afterwards, Angleton sat with Philby at a secluded table in the Mayflower Hotel Bar.

"They simply vanished like faces in the crowd," commented Philby. "No one knows where they went, or why."

Angleton looked thoughtful, then started to quote: "'The apparition of these faces in the crowd; petals on a wet, black bough.'"

Philby smiled. "Apart from Melinda, who says her husband told her he just needed a long holiday in Paris."

"How long will you be gone?"

"I suppose that depends. But I'll miss you old chap. Thanks for keeping me on my toes!"

Philby caught a shrewd glint in Angleton's eyes as he chuckled.

"And you've been keeping me on mine."

4

A gavel came down with a loud bang on a desk.

"Order!" shouted Dick White, and as the small group of men gathered in the room became silent, the sound of Big Ben chimed from a distance. White turned towards Philby. "And where exactly were you when you were first asked to investigate the identity of Homer?"

"That was three years ago," answered Philby. "How should I remember exactly?"

"Try."

Philby recollected for a moment. "Cambridge. It was our alumni reunion." He stammered as he spoke, slowing down the proceedings. White quickly became impatient.

"*Ours*, you say. And who was with you at your little class reunion that day, Mr. Philby?"

"Old friends."

"Old friends, you say. Did any of these 'old friends' include past or present members of the Foreign Office?"

"Blunt. Anthony Blunt was there. Now 'Keeper of the King's Paintings.'"

"I see. And what about Guy Burgess, or John Cairncross. Were they there?"

"I believe they were there as well."

White looked across the table at C and nodded. A murmur of voices filled the room. He turned back to Philby. "You *believe* they were there. And what of Donald Maclean? Do you believe he was there too?"

"Yes, Donald was there too." Philby stared towards a dark corner of the room, recalling with nostalgia the Cambridge garden party with his friends on a pleasant June afternoon—and toasting one another over dinner at the Trinity College High Table. White's gruff voice abruptly snapped him back into the present.

"Are you aware that John Cairncross has recently admitted to passing documents to the Soviets during the war?"

Philby sat unflinchingly as he listened to White. "I was not," he replied.

"He did so, the whole time he was at Bletchley Park in fact. MI5 found papers in his own hand to that effect in Burgess's flat after his defection. And it's now feared that he's been up to far greater mischief as well."

C abruptly stood up. "What does any of this have to do with the present case?"

White continued to gaze at Philby, undeterred. "How is it that you could have such a close relationship with these men, and yet not know they had been spying for the Soviets for some twenty years? Odd bedfellows I daresay, Mr. Philby."

"I only knew Maclean and Cairncross through Burgess. I'd scarcely seen either of them since College."

"Indeed. And yet Burgess knew Maclean well. And Burgess lived in your very house for a year, for God's sake! Did it never occur to *you* that he might be spying for the Russians?"

Philby returned White's hard stare. "Did it never occur to you? Does he seem like a secret agent, let alone a Soviet agent from whom the strictest standards would be expected? Working for a puritanical society that strictly condemns homosexuality as immoral and unacceptable? Yes, it's true Burgess has always been a close friend. Close enough indeed that I would never suspect him of duplicity."

"But what about his pro-Communist, anti-Western diatribes? Didn't you suspect something out of the ordinary?"

"No more than you obviously did. He made no more secret of his views than he did of his personal life. And yet the Foreign Office nevertheless saw fit not only to keep him on, but to assign him to their most sensitive posting." Philby gave a wry smile. "Just as, may I remind you, MI5 approved of my appointment as well."

White gave pause, seeing he was up against a wall. It was time to pull out all the stops. "That brings me to an interesting point," he pressed. "When it comes to leftist views, Burgess, Cairncross and Maclean were hardly alone at Cambridge."

"I was never a member of the Communist Party, if that's what you mean."

"Yet from 1932 to 1933, you were treasurer of the Cambridge University Socialist Society, were you not?"

"And what of it?" Philby protested. "Most students at that time were Left-wingers. Our country was teetering on the brink of all-out Fascism, for Christ's sake! There was simply the feeling that we had to stop it."

"Very conscientious of you, I'm sure. So much so that after college you married a Viennese woman who was not only an avowed Communist, but who is still a Soviet agent working from behind the Iron Curtain as we speak!"

"A youthful indiscretion."

"Only to follow that by hobnobbing with British Nazis, and the Fascists in Spain! Or was that merely cover for your Communist activity?"

"A confusing time, to be sure."

White sighed with resignation, sensing defeat. But not before one last shot. "Did you not tip off Maclean that he had been identified as 'Homer'"?

"No, I did not."

"Then who did? We know it wasn't Cairncross, as he's been under close surveillance."

"I suppose I can only assume the obvious. Since they left together, Burgess must have tipped him off."

"Then who tipped off Burgess?" White shouted in exasperation.

"Why don't you ask him?" Philby remained calm. He took out his pipe and prepared to light it.

"Please, refrain from smoking, Mr. Philby. This is a judicial enquiry."

Philby shrugged and put away his pipe. White took out a document and held it up. "I have here a memorandum from CIA deputy director Allen Dulles. It was written by an officer named Bill Harvey, whom I believe you know. It would appear you and Burgess made a particularly strong impression on his wife. Harvey has put together a number of fascinating 'coincidences' in your career. You were, for example, put in charge of the failed Volkov case in Istanbul. John Reed has been suspicious of you ever since." White paused and gazed again at Philby, who remained seemingly unperturbed. "On top of that," continued White, "you were joint commander of at least two disastrous CIA operations that led to the death or capture of almost every agent involved. You knew all about the hunt for 'Homer' and shared a house with Burgess."

C once more interrupted. "Objection! This is nothing more than McCarthyist persecution and paranoia, best left behind in the States."

"Harvey is convinced," White persisted, "that these coincidences are too many to allow for an innocent conclusion. He believes that you, Philby, are a Soviet agent guilty of high treason. And I can assure you he is not alone in that conviction."

Philby remained staid and motionless, taking White's accusations in stride.

C frowned at White. "Do you have anything more than mere circumstantial evidence to support this conclusion?"

"I believe the evidence speaks for itself."

"But is this all you've got?"

White reluctantly nodded yes.

"Then we have nothing on this man that could stand up in a court of law. Otherwise the disappearance of Burgess and Maclean has nothing to do with MI6. Philby's one of ours, and it's inconceivable that any senior member of the Secret Intelligence Service could be a traitor!"

White angrily banged his gavel on the table. "This hearing is adjourned. Good morning."

After the hearing, Philby met Aileen for lunch at The Markham Arms pub, where patrons watched a television newscast. There stood Burgess and Maclean in Moscow's Red Square, surrounded by media shouting questions. The two men wore long overcoats and furry Russian hats as they stood in the snow, and Burgess read from a prepared statement:

"...doubts as to our whereabouts and speculation about our past actions, which may again be exploited by the opponents of Anglo-Soviet understanding. We've decided to live in Moscow because it's from here we can work more effectively for world peace..."

Someone switched the channel to a cricket match. Aileen scrutinized Philby. "You're the Third Man they've been going on about, aren't you?"

Philby remained silent, watching the cricket.

"Aren't you? You're the bloody Third Man!" she shouted. "That's what you've been doing all these years, haven't you, spying for the Russians! You fucking bastard!" Aileen lifted her pint of beer from the table and splashed it in Philby's face. Then she got up and strode out of the pub as other patrons looked at Philby suspiciously. He drained his own glass and walked calmly out into the street after his wife.

5

When Philby entered MI6 headquarters, C was waiting for him at the open door. Philby smiled at Miss Pettigrew at her desk as they walked past, but she gave a disquieted look and averted her eyes.

C closed his office door and sat down at his desk. He did not offer Philby a drink. "I'm afraid I'll have to ask for your resignation. At least until this blows over." Philby nodded. "And your passport," added C. He glanced at Philby tentatively, and then smiled. "Don't worry, old boy. We still believe in you!"

Philby sat afterwards drinking alone at The Markham Arms. He held a copy of *The Times*, whose headline read:

"AMERICAN JURY CONVICTS ROSENBERGS OF NUCLEAR ESPIONAGE FOR SOVIETS; JUDGE CALLS CRIME 'WORSE THAN MURDER', SENTENCES COUPLE TO ELECTRIC CHAIR."

"Scapegoats," he muttered to himself. "Nothing but bloody scapegoats."

He found himself drifting in thought to a time years earlier, the last time he'd once possessed actual peace of mind. In his mind's eye, he stood on a bridge alone where Cambridge University spires rose behind him and distant bells tolled. From the bridge he watched carefree students punting along the river Cam below, launching him into a deep daydream.

Philby's reverie was interrupted by a report on the BBC midday radio news, where he recognized a familiar name:

"...and in other news today, Anthony Blunt, Keeper of the Royal Art Gallery, was dubbed SIR Anthony at a private ceremony at Buckingham Palace..."

Philby lifted his glass and proposed a toast to his friend. "Well done, Tony!" As he lifted his glass, he saw a man at another table across the otherwise empty pub watching him. Philby pointed his glass towards the man. "And here's to MI5!" he said before taking a deep drink.

The man's only response was his expressionless gaze.

6

During Question Time in the House of Commons, Labour MP Marcus Lipton rose from the bench.

"Has the Prime Minister made up his mind to cover up at all costs the dubious 'Third Man' activities of Mr. Harold Philby, who was at the Washington embassy a little time ago? And is he determined to stifle all discussion on the very great matters, which were evaded in the wretched White Paper and are an insult to the intelligence of the country?"

Foreign Secretary Harold Macmillan stood up to speak in response. "No evidence has been found that Philby was responsible for warning Burgess or Maclean. While in government, he carried out his duties ably and conscientiously. I have no reason to conclude that Mr. Philby has at any time betrayed the interests of the country, or to identify him with the so-called 'Third Man' if, indeed, there was one."

That afternoon flashbulbs exploded in the Philbys' living room at Drayton Gardens. A press conference was in progress as Philby stood in front of a fireplace addressing journalists. Despite his recent ordeal, he came across as impressively authoritative, charming and polite as ever. Yet as he answered the questions being posed to him, a careful observer might have noted Philby's tongue almost imperceptivity flick in and out of his cheek.

A television reporter stood up and held out a microphone. "Mr. Philby: Mr. Macmillan, the Foreign Secretary, said there was no evidence that you were the so-called 'Third Man' who allegedly tipped off Burgess and Maclean. Are you satisfied with that clearance that he gave you?"

"Yes, I am."

"Well, if there was a Third Man, were you in fact the Third Man?"

"No, I was not."

"Do you think there was one?"

"No comment."

When the conference concluded and as reporters were packing up their equipment, C walked up accompanied by Nicholas Elliott. Philby smiled when he saw them approach.

C slapped him on the back. "Well done, dear chap!"

"Thank you!"

"I have some rather good news for you. I've brought your old friend Elliott along to fill you in."

Philby looked at Elliott curiously. Elliott grinned. "Where's your local, then?"

A little later the two men sat at a quiet table by the fire in The Markham Arms, where Philby regarded Elliott with astonishment.

"Beirut?"

"We've got a vacancy there that suits your talents. It's the hotbed of intrigue in the Middle East. Both the Americans and the Soviets are competing for influence in the region and MI6 wants a presence there. You'll be our man in Beirut."

"Under what cover?"

"Journalist. I've already made all the arrangements. Your cover will be provided by *The Economist* and *The Observer*, as their 'Arab Affairs' correspondent."

Philby appeared thoughtful. "I don't suppose I can refuse."

"But of course not," laughed Elliott. He reached in his pocket and handed Philby a new passport.

At MI5 Headquarters, however, Dick White was not amused as he reviewed a list of active Secret Service agents and came across Philby's name as their MI6 man assigned to Beirut.

"Is Philby still an agent at 6?" he muttered to himself, utterly perplexed.

Philby arrived home to find Aileen packing in the bedroom. "Going somewhere?" he asked in surprise.

"Yes, Mother's. The children are already there."

Philby remained silent as their eyes met. Aileen shot him a stony look. "I've had enough, Kim. I really have. I don't know if it's because I suddenly feel I know you too little, or too much. But either way, you're a stranger to me." She angrily shut the suitcase and picked it up. He offered to help, but she refused and walked quickly out and down the stairs. Philby stood frozen a moment, listening as Aileen's footsteps descended the stairs down to the front door. Then he suddenly rushed out after her, reaching the bottom of the stairs just as she opened the door.

"Aileen!" he called, and then winced as she slammed the door in his face.

Later that same day Philby stood alone in the British Museum, where Picasso's *Guernica* was on exhibition. As he stared into the painting, his eyes glazed over with memory as he recalled the sounds of battle. But that night, he saw it all again in a vivid dream.

He sits in a car chatting and smoking with three fellow journalists as they observe a desolate, bombed out town in Spain,

1937. The night is illuminated by flashes of mortar fire, and the thunder of aircraft flying overhead.

Suddenly a piercing whine alarms the men, but before they can escape a shell explodes, leaving the car all but incinerated. As the smoke clears, Philby coughs and wipes blood from his face, only to see the charred remains of the other men. He is the only survivor.

"Bloody Fascists!"

Philby awoke with a start and sat up in bed. A feminine hand with scarlet nails reached over and caressed his face tenderly. Then he heard a familiar Russian accent.

"*Dovray otra,* Kim. Good morning! Do not worry, it was only a bad dream."

He turned to see Natasha naked in bed next to him. She rose and moved to the bathroom, where through the open door he watched her take out her lipstick and start to apply it in front of the mirror. He lay back and stared at the ceiling, his stomach knotted with angst-ridden doubt.

When he stepped out of Natasha's Soho apartment later that morning, it was raining. Natasha quickly reached outside and grabbed her umbrella, which she opened and held over Philby as he got into his car. Then she kissed him and handed him a red heart-shaped box.

"For you, Kim. I hope this will cheer you up."

As she sashayed away, he opened the box and found an assortment of fancy colored chocolates inside. He took one out and ate it, and the bittersweet cocoa warmed his heart. He smiled and took out another one.

PART V

I

Twelve years later, Dick White sat in his MI5 office sipping coffee while reading the morning paper. Things had been rather uneventful of late, and he liked it that way. But after the phone rang, years of doubt and suspicion quickly came full circle.

"A defector? What rank? What's he offering?"

At the other end of the line, British Ambassador Sir Oliver Franks sat in his office at the embassy in Washington, where two men watched him closely. "I think you may want to handle this one personally, sir." The ambassador looked up into the eyes of Anatoli Golitsin. And sitting next to him observing was James Jesus Angleton.

Nicholas Elliott was outraged as he confronted Philby at a portside café in Beirut one week later on January 22, 1963. He angrily slapped a dossier down on the table.

"You betrayed us all!"

"To betray, one must first belong," came Philby's glib reply. "I never belonged."

The two men stared at each other for a tense moment across the table.

"Nick…" began Philby.

"The name's Nicholas." Elliott opened the dossier and displayed Golitsin's evidence. "It's all here." Philby watched stone-faced as Elliott spread out a series of documents in both Russian and English, including photographs of Philby meeting with Modin and Natasha. There was also a photograph of him speaking with Maclean and Burgess at Maclean's farewell embassy reception in Washington.

Elliott squinted at Philby. "You're a ruthless bastard traitor with innocent blood on your hands! You've sold us all out." Elliott showed Philby a photograph of Agent Blackwell. "Just think of the countless agents you've betrayed over the years, men and women acting in good faith you sent straight into the arms of death. If they were lucky enough to escape years of torture in the Kremlin. You've betrayed all who ever put their faith in you."

"Not all."

"My God, how I suddenly despise you! And I hope you've still got enough decency to understand why."

"I did what was right . . . and never for self-profit. None of us did. I've remained loyal to my cause, and to the greater good."

"Bollocks!"

"When will you understand that the fight against fascism and the fight against imperialism are fundamentally the same fight? I've no more blood on my hands than any other soldier fighting for a cause he believes in."

Elliott appeared visibly disgusted. "Kim Philby, humble man of the people, staunch servant of freedom. What a load of rubbish!" He took out a further document and handed it to Philby. "We're prepared to offer you complete immunity from prosecution. Under one condition."

Philby read through the document silently as Elliott continued. "We want a full written confession at once. Then you're to return to London for extensive debriefing. And..."

Philby looked up expectantly.

"We know you're the so-called Third Man, Kim, and the ringleader of the spy ring. We know about John Cairncross, while Donald Maclean and Guy Burgess have escaped to

Moscow. But we also believe there's someone else, a fifth man in a ring of five. Someone who recruited you at Cambridge, and who's now still active as a Communist agent."

"Is that so?"

"You must reveal the identity of this agent. As well as any others you know of here and abroad."

Philby hesitated. "Very well," he said slowly. "I accept these terms, in principle. But I need a little time to think it over, and to write the confession."

"There's a reception for the new ambassador at the embassy this time tomorrow." Elliott looked at his watch. "That gives you exactly twenty-four hours. I'll expect you there at seven sharp."

Elliott reached across the table and took back the dossier, then got up and walked brusquely away. Philby stared at the papers, drained his drink, and suddenly appeared devastated as he stared into the sunset over the port.

That night Philby opened the window of his flat and looked out over the Port of Beirut. A strong sea breeze blew the curtains wildly. His attention was caught by a sliding noise from inside the flat, and he turned to see a letter being slid through the space beneath the door. Then he saw the shadow of two feet moving quickly away. He rushed to the door and opened it, but only heard footsteps descending the stairs. He picked up the letter and moved back to the window just in time to see a figure exit the building below and disappear into the night shadows.

Finally, he looked at the envelope. On it the initials 'KP' were handwritten in red ink.

2

The next evening Elliott stood at the entrance of the British Embassy in Beirut, where he listened to a string quartet performing Vivaldi's "Winter" at the elegant reception inside. He looked nervously at his watch. It was a quarter past seven.

Just then an aide strode up to him. "Sir, we've got word a Russian freighter's making an unscheduled arrival at port. It's just now docking."

"Contact Lebanese Security at once!" shouted Elliott. Within minutes the embassy gates swung open as a motorcade of military vehicles sped through, with Elliott in the leading car escorted by Lebanese police. When they arrived at the waterfront, Elliott saw Philby lying face down among the bodies of Lebanese soldiers shot by Russian snipers. All seemed deadly silent beneath the looming freighter *Dolmatova*, apart from the distant sound of a muezzin chanting the morning prayer.

Philby stirred as sailors called to him from the freighter, and with an effort managed to pull himself up and stagger down the landing. The embassy guards, led by Elliot, fired at him but were held at bay by Russian snipers returning fire from above.

When he reached the ship, Philby was quickly pulled on board with the help of ropes. The sailors hastily hauled in the moorings, and the freighter pulled away just as Elliot arrived at the water's edge.

Philby watched from the deck in silence as the freighter moved slowly away from port. Across the water, he made eye contact with Elliott, who watched helplessly as Philby slipped away into the open sea.

Elliott looked down into the dark water. "Damn," he uttered, and then turned his back to Philby and walked back toward the car.

In the alley behind him, a cigarette butt hit the ground and was stubbed out by the toe of a boot. Out stepped Angleton, who stood a while watching the ship move out to sea in the distance, until it eventually mingled with the hundreds of other vessels drifting through the busy port.

"Well played, comrade," he chuckled. Then he vanished back into the shadows.

EPILOGUE

Harold 'Kim' Philby presided over the notorious 'Cambridge Five' spy ring that penetrated the British Secret Intelligence Service (MI6), passing vital information to the Soviets for decades.

After escaping from Beirut aboard the Soviet freighter *Dolmatova* on January 23, 1963, Philby defected to the Soviet Union to join Donald Maclean and Guy Burgess in Moscow, where they lived out the rest of their lives in exile.

The man who had recruited the young men at Cambridge University while teaching there was Sir Anthony Blunt, later a distinguished art historian who served the Queen for many years as Surveyor of the Queen's Pictures. When Blunt's identity as a member of the spy ring was finally revealed in 1979 by Prime Minister Thatcher, he was formally stripped of his knighthood.

Philby became celebrated as a national Soviet hero, even having his portrait featured on a USSR postage stamp. When he died in Moscow in 1988, he was given a hero's state funeral.

None of the Cambridge Five were ever prosecuted.

THE CALL

(Adapted from *Before I Sleep: A Memoir of Travel and Reconciliation*)

We shall not cease from exploration
And the end of all our exploring
Will be to arrive where we started
And know the place for the first time.
                    —T.S. Eliot, from *Four Quartets*

THE LATE AFTERNOON SUN had finally impaled the English clouds, revealing wisps of blue sky after a dull grey morning of cold drizzle. A spring breeze scented with jasmine wafted its way through an open window, where nascent sunlight transformed raindrops lining the panes into pearls of liquid silver. The light suffused my tiny student room with sudden warmth, and through the window across the desk I watched a moving grove of bright umbrellas transfigure into human faces along the street below.

I sat back in my chair and took a deep breath. The lowering clouds in the distance swirled above a row of red-bricked Victorian rooftops, and the fresh air and sunlight seemed a welcome sign that a break from academic work was in order. The phone suddenly announced its presence like a herald, and I was pleased to hear my mother's voice, although surprised to hear from her so unexpectedly outside of our usual Sunday chat. But her voice revealed that something was not quite right. Something, in fact, that would completely transform my life.

After I hung up the phone, I sat back in a daze. On the walls of my room the orange glimmer of sunset painted a glowing patina of serrated light before fading with dusk to a dim, crimson glow. A drop of warm dampness upon my arm startled me from deep reverie. I had not noticed the tears in my eyes, through which the growing darkness painted for my imagination an impressionistic forest of blurry images. I switched on the lamp by the phone and quickly dialed a number.

When Brad found me at a table in the Gloucester Arms pub half an hour later, I was studying a shamrock drawn upon the creamy top of a cool thick pint of dark stout. He sat down across from me.

"You okay?"

As I looked up I realized too late my face was streaked once more with tears, and my friend was taken aback. We'd known each other several years now, fellow Yanks at Oxford who had connected as being both from the South—with all its associated idiosyncrasies that few other compatriots seemed to appreciate.

"I just heard from my father..." I hardly spoke the words before I found it difficult to go on. "I think I told you once that I never knew him."

Brad nodded thoughtfully. "Yes, I remember your mentioning that."

"Not since I was three years old at least, when he left." I paused again to regain composure as Brad waited. As I struggled to express my predicament, I felt a profound sense of gratitude simply for having a friend there to listen. I drank a deep sip of beer, savoring its cool, bitter taste as someone put a song on the jukebox behind us and a heavy rock ballad started to play. I took a deep breath and continued.

"My mother called to say she'd heard from him. Or from his family, rather. They said my father's on his death bed dying of lung cancer. The doctor says he's got less than a week to live, and now he wants to speak with me before he dies."

I had told my mother that I would accept my father's call. She said they had asked about the time difference and when would be the best time for him to call me, and I asked her to set the time for three in the afternoon the next day. After I'd recounted this, I lost my composure once more, as the significance of this fateful news fully manifested itself in thought. Once I had recovered, Brad's next comment threw me for a loop.

"You have to go see him."

"What?"

"You should get on the next flight home to the States and meet your father before he dies. You'll always regret it if you don't."

I told him I had already suggested this to my mother, but she was adamant that I should not do so. She wondered why I should I fly across the ocean to meet a father who, as it turned out, had spent the last three decades in

Hot Springs, Arkansas—just up the road from our home in Little Rock—without making any effort to contact me. That point so angered me that any desire to meet this permanently absent biological father (apart from a quick chat by phone for the sake of closure) felt completely removed.

But Brad was likewise insistent that I should meet my birth father. He explained that not doing so when I had this one chance would haunt me for the rest of my life. And he was speaking from experience, having lost his own father. The only way I could ever confront the lifelong sense of emptiness I had endured was to finally meet, just once before he died, the father I had never known. This was the only way I might achieve a true sense of closure.

By the end of the evening, I had made my decision. I would travel home to meet my father.

The next day brought a fine May afternoon, the kind of day that makes a whole year's worth of English weather worth the wait. I walked down the street to a small park in Wellington Square and sat in the grass beneath an ancient, sprawling oak. I looked at my watch. Forty-five minutes. In forty-five minutes, the phone on my desk would be ringing, and on the other end of the line would be the voice of my father. A voice I had never known in my conscious life. What would it sound like? What would he say? What would *I* say? These were questions that must have been buried within my subconscious my whole lifetime up to that very moment—along with the ever-haunting question of his permanent absence. Everything else that had preoccupied my mind only a day earlier, before my mother's call, had suddenly vanished. It was as if all my daily preoccupations, the day to day reality that normally seemed so damned important, had melted away in the mists of memory: memories of forgotten mystery, of a lifetime unaware I was waiting all along for this one phone call—as if all my waking, superficial being of daily trivial, egoistic concerns and petty pursuits—had met an abrupt, untimely death, swallowed by the depths of a forgotten consciousness suddenly now ripped to the surface. Memories of earliest childhood, long forgotten, flooded my mind, as a lifetime of experiences flashed before my mind's eye like the fabled moment of death.

In the park, the summer roses were in full bloom—yellow, red and white. I walked over to a rose bush and inhaled, slowly, deeply and deliberately, its pungent sweetness. As I bent down and smelled each rose in turn, their redolence transported me to a place far way. A place all but forgotten outside of dreams.

Sunlight streamed through parting clouds after a heavy rain, and the humid Delta air hung thick beneath the ancient live oak. From below, its leaves glistened like emerald stars illuminating a panoply of green sky. The tree's gnarled roots seemed magical, grasping outward from the trunk like multifarious tentacles, their various crevices now filled with rainwater that I imagined as tiny oceans filled with fish. And that reminded me that my cousin had promised to take me fishing down at the pond as soon as the storm broke.

The sound of clippers stirred me from my reverie, and I looked to see my grandmother resuming her work in the garden. She was pruning the rose bushes. I ran over to her, delighting in the flowers' radiant colors after the rain: pink, white, yellow and scarlet red, all dripping with the sunlit sparkle of rainwater. I pulled a rose toward me and inhaled the sweet scent. From beneath her old wide-brimmed straw hat, my grandmother's eyes glanced quickly at me with a look of concern.

"Now you be careful of those thorns, they're sharper than they look."

"Yes, ma'am," I answered perfunctorily, carefully allowing my hand to move backward with the stem until it found a smooth place between two thorns. My grandmother hadn't missed a beat, remaining engrossed in her gardening. She had moved over to the next rose bush, oblivious to the iridescent halo of butterflies flitting among the flowers.

I watched her curiously, always fascinated by her solemn work ethic. "Where's Mama?"

"Up in Paragould. But she'll be home directly, I reckon." My grandmother remained a study in concentration as she carefully trimmed another rose bush, like a sculptor at work in the studio. It was clear that this was the best answer I was going to get today, so I ran along to the swing in the front yard. A window air-conditioning unit whirred to life, and I knew my grandfather must be up from his nap. I excitedly jumped from the swing and ran across the yard as fast as my three year old legs would carry me, up the wooden front steps and into the front hall of the old house. The living room door was closed to seal in the precious cool air, and I could already hear my grandfather inside tapping his pipe on the glass ashtray. I opened the door and enjoyed the sensation of feeling the stuffy heat of the hall mix with the frigid cold air streaming from the air conditioner. In the living room, my grandfather had just settled into his new reclining chair by the window, and as usual focused immediately on filling his pipe from a small red tin can of Prince Albert tobacco.

In the thin sliver of natural light slanting through the window was caught a galaxy of dust motes orbiting my grandfather's face.

They vanished suddenly as he switched on the lamp.

"Hey, buddy!" he mumbled affably upon seeing me, holding the pipe stem to his mouth with one hand while lighting a wooden match with the other. After a few puffs the tobacco in his pipe glowed crimson, as several sparks flew off in various directions— the sort of sparks that had, to my grandmother's chagrin, left burn marks on the furniture and floors, and that would one day set the whole house ablaze, burning it completely to the ground along with everything in it.

But now I sat contentedly on the old red couch next to my grandfather in his chair, savoring the smell of his tobacco and the gentle hum of the air conditioner that rendered silent the motion of tree branches and flowers swaying in a hot breeze outside the window. I still wasn't sure where my mother was, but here inside with my grandfather, I felt safe.

As I sat in the rose-filled garden of Wellington Square lost in these thoughts, I nearly lost track of the time. 2:55! The call from my father was set for 3:00, so I ran around the corner and upstairs to my room and sat staring, breathless, at the phone on my desk. At exactly 3:00, it rang. When I picked up the receiver, the voice on the other end was that of my birth father.

I tried to act and sound as if this were just any casual phone conversation with an old acquaintance. I could never have prepared myself for the emotional maelstrom upon hearing, as a grown man, the voice of the father I'd never known. But it was a voice in pain, this I could tell. He was in the advanced stage of lung cancer, and—whether because of this or the context or perhaps a bit of both— his words did not come easily. I found myself doing most of the talking, and what he wanted to know was how I'd spent the last 30 years of my life. At one point he abruptly changed the subject.

"Do you smoke?" he asked.

"Only sometimes, when I've had a few drinks."

"Don't," he said, and as if by illustration fell into a fit of coughing. "It's not worth it, let me tell you. I quit smoking ten years ago, but it still caught up with me now."

I could tell it was getting difficult for him to continue the conversation, and I recalled Brad's advice that I must try to meet my father at all cost. But despite my fear of rejection even at the last, I told him I wanted to fly home to Arkansas and meet him. He simply answered that it wouldn't be necessary. Yet there was something in his voice that seemed uncertain. So I said again that I really meant it—I wanted us to meet while we still could.

"If you want to come," he answered, "we'll be glad to have you."

Since I knew that in a matter of days it would be too late, I went immediately to a travel agency and booked the trip. During the flight home, I thought mostly about what I would say to my adoptive father, Russell. I had asked my mother to ensure that he was present for dinner on the night before my journey to Hot Springs, and I knew I had this one chance to express things just right. The weight of this challenge felt almost overwhelming; in our whole life together as a family, the subject of my biological father had not come up even once in conversation—not even after Dad formally adopted me. But I'd always felt it as a topic hovering just beneath the surface, waiting for the moment when it (or my birth father himself) would suddenly and unexpectedly appear. And that moment was now.

As we sat around the formal dining table enjoying casual conversation about my latest adventures abroad, the sense of expectancy was palpable. Everyone knew why I suddenly returned home, but the onus was on me to bring it up. Finally, I did. I explained that I'd learned my birth father was on his death bed with a matter of days to live, and that I'd decided I must meet him before he died to close this empty gap in my life. Then I turned and looked at Dad.

"I want you to know that I'm only meeting him because he's my biological father, and that I have to do this before he dies. But it's you I consider my real father. You're the only one who was there for me. You've always been, and always will be, my only true father."

Dad nodded with understanding. "You're doing the right thing, son," he said. "You need this sense of closure."

My old school friend Robert offered to travel with me from Little Rock to Hot Springs so I wouldn't have to journey there alone. We drove up the day before my appointment with my father and stayed the night in a hotel on Lake Hamilton. The next morning we drove to the house where my father had lived with his girlfriend and her family for many years. I was greeted in the front yard by a man of about my own age named Randall.

"I know exactly what you're experiencing," he said. "I met my own birth father later in life too." By the time we entered the house, Randall explained how he was brought up in turn by my biological father like a son of his own. (My father had otherwise had no further children.) I was still processing this when I was greeted at the door by Randall's mother, Monica. She welcomed me graciously and led me into the living room, where several other women—including Randall's wife and sister—waited.

"He's in the back room," said Monica. "He's expecting you." Robert waited with Randall as I followed Monica into the back of the house. We entered the back room and there he was, sitting in a chair waiting for me. Randall had quickly explained that the only reason my father wasn't in a hospital bed hooked up to a ventilator was that he'd wanted to meet me with dignity. So they'd had the machine set up here, next to his chair.

Monica showed me to a seat and then discreetly left the room. I didn't know what to say, but I knew an attempt at small talk would seem, under the circumstances, bathetic. But he spoke first.

"You're studying English literature?"

I could tell from his voice that his health had already declined rapidly in the three days since we had last spoken.

"Yes, I'm studying medieval and Renaissance drama." Then to my surprise he began to recite Chaucer in Middle English:

Whan that April with his showres soote
The droughte of March hath perced to the roote...

I suddenly realized the room we were in was a private study full of books. There were books everywhere, with every imaginable title from Dostoevsky to Chomsky to a treatise on the art of growing marijuana. He told me of his archaeological research in England and showed me photographs from his travels. He then commended me for my academic success, and said he'd been pleased to hear it.

"I guess you gave me some good genes," I said.

"You got your genes from your mother."

Then he finally asked me about her. I told him what a wonderful mother she had been to me, and how she'd encouraged and supported me in my every endeavor throughout my life. Suddenly, he began coughing violently, and Monica rushed into the room to adjust the ventilator.

I looked into his eyes and was struck by a strange sense of familiarity, and then realized his eyes seemed the mirror image of my own. Yet, they now betrayed something else too—something he would finally express before we said goodbye. I told my father simply how glad I was finally to have met him. I told him that I would one day write about our meeting, so that this occasion (and he) would not be forgotten. It was now my turn to quote poetry, and I recalled two lines which seemed to fit the sentiment perfectly:

> So long as men can breathe, or eyes can see,
>   So long lives this, and this gives life to thee.

My father nodded. Then I said, "I want you to know that as you are my father, I love you."

Just as I turned to leave, he seemed to be struggling to summon up one last word.

"Don't die bitter," he said.

Then he looked deeply into my eyes before saying the last words I would ever hear from him: "I regret."

With this he abruptly dropped his chin to his chest with a look of final resignation. As I turned away my eyes filled with tears, and when they saw my face the women in the room began to weep. Randall accompanied me outside where Robert was waiting at the car, and I thanked him for helping make my visit such a warm one. Then Monica came out and said she had something for me from my father.

"He insisted on this," she said, handing me a check to cover the cost of my trip from London. On the check he had written: "For love and travel."

The next day Randall called to say that my father had died that night. He had left me all his books. He'd been worried what to do with them and at the end said he was pleased to find he had a son who read.

"He spent the last few days of his life trying to tie up all the loose ends before you arrived," Randall explained. "We told him he should just rest and save energy, and that we'd take care of everything. Yet he insisted, and just kept saying—*but I have promises to keep.*"

I smiled, and said I'd be happy to have my father's books. Then I recited softly to myself: *And miles to go before I sleep.*

RING OF FIVE
Further Reading and Sources

The author drew from these sources as well as media reports for some of the facts that informed the writing of "Ring of Five." While based on a true story, "Ring of Five" is a work of fiction.

Borovik, Genrikh. *The Philby Files: The Secret Life of Master Spy Kim Philby*. Boston: Little, Brown & Company, 1994.

Carter, Miranda. *Anthony Blunt: His Lives*. New York: Farrar, Straus and Giroux, 2002.

Fisher, John. *Burgess and Maclean*. London: Robert Hale, Ltd., 1977.

Hamrick, s.j. *Deceiving the Deceivers*. New Haven: Yale University Press, 2004.

Knightley, Phillip. *The Master Spy: The Story of Kim Philby*. New York: Vintage, 1990.

Macintyre, Ben. *A Spy Among Friends: Kim Philby and the Great Betrayal*. New York: Crown, 2014. (Afterward by John le Carré)

Milne, Tim. *Kim Philby: The Unknown Story of the KGB's Master Spy*. London: Biteback Publishing, 2014.

Page, Bruce, David Leitch, and Phillip Knightley. *Philby: The Spy Who Betrayed a Generation*. London: Trafalgar Square, 1968.

Philby, Kim. *My Silent War: The Autobiography of a Spy*. New York: Modern Library, 2002. (Foreword by Graham Greene)

Trahair, Richard C.S. and Robert Miller. *Encyclopedia of Cold War Espionage, Spies, and Secret Operations*. New York: Enigma Books, 2012.

West, Nigel and Oleg Tsarev. *The Crown Jewels: The British Secrets at the Heart of the KGB Archives*. New Haven: Yale University Press, 1999.

FRANK H. THURMOND grew up in Little Rock, Arkansas, and holds graduate degrees in English from Southern Methodist University and Oxford University. In addition to writing, he is a musician and filmmaker, and is currently working on a feature film adaptation of his novella *Ring of Five*.

Thurmond is a Visiting Assistant Professor of English at the University of Arkansas at Little Rock.

This book was set in 13pt Adobe Jenson Pro
Interior layout by Jeremy Kistler

www.ingramcontent.com/pod-product-compliance
Lightning Source LLC
Chambersburg PA
CBHW020656260626
47157CB00008B/3050